THE
HORSE KEEPER

THE
HORSE KEEPER

A. R. FORTE

Copyright © 2013 A. R. Forte

The moral right of the author has been asserted.

Apart from any fair dealing for the purposes of research or private study, or criticism or review, as permitted under the Copyright, Designs and Patents Act 1988, this publication may only be reproduced, stored or transmitted, in any form or by any means, with the prior permission in writing of the publishers, or in the case of reprographic reproduction in accordance with the terms of licences issued by the Copyright Licensing Agency. Enquiries concerning reproduction outside those terms should be sent to the publishers.

Matador
9 Priory Business Park,
Wistow Road, Kibworth Beauchamp,
Leicestershire. LE8 0RX
Tel: (+44) 116 279 2299
Fax: (+44) 116 279 2277
Email: books@troubador.co.uk
Web: www.troubador.co.uk/matador

ISBN 978 1780883 557

British Library Cataloguing in Publication Data.
A catalogue record for this book is available from the British Library.

Printed and bound in the UK by TJ International, Padstow, Cornwall
Typeset in 11pt Minion Pro by Troubador Publishing Ltd, Leicester, UK

Matador is an imprint of Troubador Publishing Ltd

CONTENTS

Introduction.
Rambling back. June 1868.

Chapter 1	1
Chapter 2	5
Chapter 3 *Whispers of a delta breeze. May 1858.*	25
Riding on the wind.	30
Chapter 4 *I don't pree-fess to know.*	39
Chapter 5 *Sensual pleasures of a bodily kind.*	47
Chapter 6 *The man who stole a thief.*	55
Peach blossoms and pink confetti.	64
Chapter 7	69
Chapter 8	74

Chapter 9	81
Chapter 10	86
Chapter 11	91
Chapter 12 *A boy, a torch and a barn.*	101
Chapter 13	108
Chapter 14	124
Chapter 15	133
Chapter 16	138
Chapter 17	143
Chapter 18 *The General and the telegrapher.*	148
Chapter 19 *A General and a long speech.*	155
Chapter 20 *The call of the hallowed wind.*	168

At the grand old age of seventy two,
Blucher fought at Waterloo.
Napoleon made war an art,
But Wellington was very smart.
William Wallace fought in tartan,
And Leonidas was a Spartan.
Marching off to fife and drum.
The enemy is on the run.
A soldier's life is death or glory,
But that's not the only story.
Beneath the cloak of glory gained,
Hides the sword of shame and pain.
Black flowers sprung from the bud,
When Cromwell signed his name in blood.
And who's that knocking on deaths door.
The dreaded ghost of CIVIL WAR…

A.R. Forte.

INTRODUCTION

Rambling back. June 1868.

Luke gently reigned in the train of young horses as he finally pulled his own horse to a halt when they reached the hilltop. He looked down into the valley and was pleased with what he saw. The deep, lush greenery around the dense, low slung meadow was perfect for grazing and also the canopy of trees provided an excellent place to camp for the night. He looked over his shoulder and said to the six fillies and three young males, "well, boys and gals, looks like we gotta damn good place to rest up an' feed." The horses responded to the tenderness in his voice by moving their beautiful heads in unison. They were indeed a fine bunch and Luke had paid the rancher cash for them, without even bothering to haggle and barter. After all, Luke knew exactly what he was looking for and he would certainly be doing business with Tex Bodell again. The only man that knew more about horses than Luke was about a bus ride away and Luke was looking forward to handing these gems to his friend and mentor.

Before descending into the valley he took a sweeping look around. Luke loved the land and he felt part of its invisible ambience. He loved every mountain, skyline, valley, glade, river and body of water. It flowed through his soul like an eternal stream of creativity and growth. So as he gently pulled and tugged at the long line to lead his obedient fold down into the valley, he could not have been prepared for what was about to happen. When they approached the meadow he received a stark warning. As he dismounted and led the troupe into the deep grass, his own horse became disturbed and immediately after, the rest of the horses began to fret and fidget. They were afraid of something and Luke felt the cold clasp of fear suddenly grab his spine.

"Easy, easy boys and gals, there's nothin' round here to be afraid of," he said.

He tethered the train to a solitary tree further back from the glade and walked briskly under the canopy of trees with the grass lashing around his boots, determined to get to the root of the horses' disturbance.

He did not have to look far to find out what it was.

As soon as he entered under the shadows of the trees and at exactly at the same instant, he felt his boot kick something and his eagle eye caught something to his left. The broken artillery piece was covered in ivy and deep undergrowth, but he knew a Napoleon when he saw one. Looking down he noticed with horror that his boot had caught a human skull. As his eyes adjusted to the shade, the scene told him what must have happened here, a few years before. The tangle of bones grew into a more concentrated conglomeration in the centre of the glade. The rotting, mildew ridden fabric, some blue some grey, told Luke that this had been the scene of a fierce engagement. Mother Nature had tried to weave her mysterious web over this dastardly deed, but she had not had enough time to cover them with her veil of green. The barrels of the broken Parrot cannons protruded from the bracken and tall weeds, pointing in all directions. Luke pictured the scene as much as the macabre evidence graphically informed him. Rebel soldiers descending from all sides, whooping and screaming the Rebel yell. Disciplined, but terrified Union boys cutting them down with musket fire and decapitating bodies with canister and shot from the artillery pieces, and finally the inevitable hand to hand fight, with bayonet and sword. Luke suddenly felt as though he was trespassing and intruding on a hallowed and sacred place.

He turned around and walked back. Looking towards the sky with tears in his eyes he asked, "Why, why did you let this happen? Why did you not intervene and stop it, why?" He unhitched the horses that appeared to be quietly observing his distress and said, "Well, boys and gals, looks like we're gonna' have to find somewhere else tonight."

He finally found a suitable place to camp about an hour later, on the other side of the hill that rose from the back of the hidden and beautifully camouflaged cemetery. The horses had been quiet as they approached the next cluster of trees and dense shrubbery, and Luke took stock of their manner and countenance in quiet interest and relief.

He woke early the next morning and after brewing up a strong pot of coffee and making sure that the horses had been watered by a nearby stream, he saddled up his own horse and made ready to leave. Luke was nowhere near as strong and as powerfully built as his mentor and benefactor, but he was tall, lean and athletic and had incredible stamina and endurance. Very few men could spend as much time in the saddle and cover such vast tracks of land as he could in a day. If he had not decided to take this overland route back to the ranch and had stayed on the dusty roads, he would not have stumbled upon the tragic reminder that a terrible war had scarred and tarnished this benign and fertile land. But this was no time for regrets and pondering over unfortunate incidents. This was the time Luke loved best about his forays and travels; rambling back. He was rambling back under his own steam. The deal had been done and he had bought merchandise well above his expectations. But, above all of this he knew that his mentor would be pleased and that warmed his heart. He was looking forward to the twin boys running towards him across the yard, and carrying each one as they hung onto his legs. And, of course, he could sure use a hot meal and warm bed.

It was a magnificent sunrise that greeted Luke as he negotiated the final boulders and rocks when he reached the top of the final hill that overlooked the ranch. The sun was glowing a bright orange and scarlet, and violet cloud formations stretched across the horizon like branches of atmospheric trees. He looked down onto the ranch far below and the rooster called as if it had been waiting for him to arrive. Smoke spiralled up from the chimney of the ranch house and he knew that Belinda was busy at work in the kitchen. The twins, Kyle and Virgil would still be sound asleep in their bunks. Luke doted on the twins and they saw him more like a big brother, rather than a surrogate uncle. The war had cheated Luke out of his own childhood, the very fibre of his youth and he knew that he owed everything to the fiery, tough and mysterious loner that had given him a lifeline. He was about as content as a young man could be, considering all of the horror, fear and gut wrenching injustice he had seen and lived through, in his desperate former life.

He smiled, then looked over his shoulder and winked at the train of fine beasts. His heart swelled with pride as he loudly announced, "Well, boys and gals, it's time to meet your new master and ma' boss."

His gaze then turned down towards the labyrinth of stables, barns and pens. He knew that somewhere amongst that tangle of wood, delivering newly born foals, or feeding and attending to sickly fillies and caring for the animals that he had been born

CHAPTER 1

Wayne tied the laces of his heavy boots and stood up from the steps of the porch. The boots felt strange and the crisp grey uniform felt like dry cardboard. The Colonel had told him to report to the General in the morning and had assured him not to worry, as the General only wanted a casual chat. Wayne knew the General from many bloody battlefields, body and soul breaking marches, through dust, rain, blazing sun and freezing cold. But as he walked across the dusty square he wondered what the General could want with him. He knew the old man was pompous, theatrical and prone to long elaborate speeches, punctuated with well placed metaphors. But what was there to say that they did not already know, share and suffer. These thoughts were still swimming around inside his head as he knocked on the Generals office door.

"Come in," a gruff voice said loudly.

As Wayne walked into the room, a huge imposing figure stood up from behind a desk. It took Wayne a while for his eyes to adjust to the relative darkness, compared to the blinding sunshine that splayed into the room through a dusty window.

"Ah, private Rawlins I believe, well, well, please take a seat my brave boy."

Wayne sat down on a rickety old chair facing the General who sat down himself. "I suppose you're wondering why I called for you," said the General.

"Yes sir, the Colonel told me you wanted to speak to me last night sir."

"Hope he told you it was informal and not over discipline or rules."

"He did sir," said Wayne, barely hiding the curiosity in his voice.

"Damn good soldier, Colonel Williams. Wish we had him in one of our brigades at Antietam, or Fredericksburg, or Chancellorsville for that matter," said the General.

"It's a pleasure working under Colonel Williams sir, he's a veteran of…"

The old man interrupted sharply, and a wry smile came across his face, as he said, "just like us, my brave boy, just like us… War torn, shattered veterans." Only now did the General look down on the papers on his desk, then look up at Wayne with a pain and anguish in his eyes that defied description.

"I see that you've been with us from the beginning… Four years from the beginning that we all thought would end within months. How wrong we all were, how wrong." He suddenly became aware of Wayne's anxious gaze and said more cordially, "I bet you wonder how you've survived all of those infernal battles, when so many like yourself perished and died in such horrible bloodshed."

"I do sir, I do, every day and night, there's no escape from it."

The General butted in again and Wayne got the impression that the old man needed somebody to talk to, and to vent a pent up anger, which he had been brooding over. "From Bull run to Fredericksburg, Antietam to Chancellorsville… From the Pickett, Pettigrew, Trimble charge at Gettysburg. To the terrible Wilderness battle... Where did you get wounded by the way?"

"I was finally felled at the Bloody angle massacre in front of Spotsylvania Court house. I was dug out from a pile of Yankees who were so mutilated that their blood soaked my uniform red through... I cannot believe I am here in front of you sir, I cannot believe I'm still alive... I was near General Pettigrew when he was shot sir, as we pulled away from the field at Gettysburg. He could have saved himself, but he made sure we all got across a deep ford and took a Yankee bullet trying to cross behind us."

"Damn fine General, Pettigrew, an intellectual. I knew him personally, can't believe how he was taken after surviving that charge... I almost forgot the main reason I wanted to see you... Why were you the only western boy from your town drafted into an eastern army? The Colonel mentioned something about handling horses."

Suddenly Wayne became self conscious and slightly nervous about this question and had to think carefully before he answered it, as the General listened with interest.

"Well sir, I've always loved horses from a young age and was given an ability, or gift to train and break most wild horses, given time... Er, my reputation for this got around over some time and we kept horses on my father's ranch anyway... So I was lucky enough to do a job that I liked... When all of the boys in Rogersville were volunteering and being drafted into the Western armies, I got a job taking several big batches of horses up to Virginia and training and breaking horses that had been herded in from everywhere. Horses were being killed and worked to death hauling artillery and wagons at a far worse rate than in the West, and were needed badly."

"What do you put this talent down to?" asked the General.

"It's quite simple sir. Every horse has its own personality, its own character, I believe... You have to get to know each one individually, then befriend it. And then it's a matter of earning its trust. Even the wildest and most ferocious ones can be trained, if they are handled properly... Some folks that think they know horses know nothing. A horse is no dumb beast sir, it has feelings, just like us."

Just then somebody knocked on the door.

"Enter," said the General.

Colonel Williams entered the room and said proudly, "Sir, you ordered me to inform you as soon as the next batch of horses were brought in. Well, they're here sir, and there's some real beauties among 'em."

"Thank you Colonel. Well my last horse was blown from underneath me by a cannon ball. Private Rawlins, I want you to choose one for me, and do your work on it. Then call for me when you think I can handle it."

Training and dealing with the horses that were brought in had been Wayne's prime job around Headquarters after he was brought down from the field hospital. The wound in his leg had healed quite well, but he now had a slight limp and the muscle that the musket ball had pierced could sometimes give him sudden spasms of pain in the night. Headquarters was nothing more than an old deserted outpost, with a few dilapidated wooden buildings, barns and stables huddled together, surrounding a dusty square.

The other boys that worked around Headquarters were all crammed into a ramshackle bunkhouse, with broken and missing slates. Wayne had been fortunate enough to be put into a small but dry room at the back of the stables, where he was in close proximity and smell of his beautiful beasts.

The General had turned out to be a superb administrator. Everybody, including the dispossessed slaves who worked as washerwomen and seamstresses were fed on fresh potatoes, corn bread and a quite palatable stew that the General himself ate in copious amounts. The General's staff had managed to check most of the graft and thievery that was infamous around army supply points. In short, if anybody were caught they would be shot, was the maxim. Would be surreptitious business was soon quelled by this ethic.

There were about two hundred and sixty of them manning the camp, and Wayne knew most of them. Some of them had even been in the same amount of battles as him. And all of them had a great deal of respect for the western boy, who had been drafted over to take care of horses, but had fought side by side with them, suffering the same dangers and conditions. Wayne would stand by the stables every day and watch with pity as old men, teenage boys and poor simpletons in grey cotton uniforms pass through the depot. Going to shore up broken and battered armies, that was dying a slow and painful death. Wayne knew that most of them would never return.

CHAPTER 2

The new batch of horses were indeed a magnificent collection. Twenty-four well fed and watered wild beasts. They had been hidden in a corner of a vast plantation down in Georgia in lieu of being sold for an extortionate price after the war. General Hardee's men had discovered them by accident as they were negotiating a surprise attack on a probing Federal cavalry patrol. For Wayne it was love at first sight, and they were all his to train tame and ultimately make obedient servants to their master.

He soon picked out a powerful and athletic brown stallion for the General. The beast was young and wild and had the character of a cock-sure youth that could face any challenge. The day after they had been brought in Wayne was leaning against the fence of the big pen behind the stables observing them and their ways. He became vaguely aware of somebody watching him. He turned to see a wiry youth standing sheepishly looking at him from under the brim of a big brown hat.

"Whatchu want boy," said Wayne sharply.

"Mr. Rawlins... I, I, I've been sent by Colonel Williams to w, w, work for yah."

Wayne suddenly realised that his own manner had been unreasonable and replied, "Whatshu name boy?"

"Luke, sir."

"How old are yah Luke?"

"Fifteen, s, sixteen next month sir."

Wayne wondered if the boy's stammer was real or born of nerves.

"Well Luke, one thing we gotta get straight for a start… I ain't no mister and I ain't no sir, call me Wayne. Do yah know much 'bout horses Luke?"

"Not much, but I wanna learn, I sure wanna own one too someday."

"Why did the Colonel choose yah Luke? He's got 'bout fifty other boys doing duties round here. Wouldn't guarding stores and prisoners be a lot easier?"

"I volunteered, I heard a lot about yah from some of the boys."

Wayne thought a while and adopted a more friendly and quieter tone. "Yeh, some of us have been together for three or four years, we all know we sure are lucky to still be here in one piece, or with pieces of us missin.'"

Deep inside Wayne felt like the pieces of a vast jigsaw puzzle, broken and scattered. With pieces missing in an emotional swamp of turmoil, battles, hunger, thirst and fear. And soul breaking marches over unfamiliar terrain, with the ever-present enemy close.

At night a lot of the boys would sit around a big campfire at the back of the bunkhouse exchanging stories. These gatherings had become standard practice over the months and Wayne would always attend for a few hours. He liked to listen rather than have any input, because it gave him a peculiar comfort to know he wasn't alone.

One of the boys who had been a brewer in another incarnation had got a regular brewery going in one of the sheds. The beer he turned out was cloudy and deceptively strong, but it was as good as anything that self-appointed experts on beer had tasted.

General Officers had not encouraged these beer sodden gatherings, but had turned a blind eye to them. This clandestine band of brothers deserved some form of respite from a war that had turned brother against brother, friend against friend. There was no hatred for the boys in blue who were being replaced and killed wholesale by General Lee's formidable and daring army of Northern Virginia. The hatred was in the hearts of the men who wielded the power, who pitted farm boy from Arkansas against clerk from Maine. Who spoke boldly of bloody consequences and reprisals, but would never be bold enough themselves to pick up a musket or man an artillery piece.

Even the most humblest among these gatherings had done their piece, had parried and ridden the punches of a far bigger and better equipped army. It was of small comfort to them that the Federal armies of East and West despised and detested each other far more than they did the Johnnie Reb. It had not helped them that the Billy Yank revered and admired rebel Generals more than their own.

Because when the armies collided in battle, in fields, over hills, in forest and swamp, every veteran knew that the opposition would fight with pugnacious ferocity.

All in all camp life was relatively pleasant at best and bearable at worst. Guarding Federal prisoners that were to be transported to prison camps, or loading and unloading stores that had to be quickly transported up to Petersburg by wagon and rail, was a far better proposition than hard fighting. Nobody wanted to cause any unnecessary fuss or problems, or draw unwanted attention to themselves. The Federal prisoners were kept in a big, semi derelict jailhouse and most of the boys treated them well. They would exchange stories and the Union boys would all agree that they had never served under a more hard fighting and demanding General than the quiet and unassuming General Grant. Just like their Officers these boys had been suspicious of this Ulysses. S Grant, and when he was brought over from the west to take up command the question across the whole army was – Who is this Grant? When Grant had pulled out the forty big siege guns guarding Washington and put them up on front line duty, complete with their crews, and drafted all of the cavalry guarding Washington into front line infantry units, he was only starting to make his presence felt. This had delighted the army of the Potomac veterans. The rebels probably had a better insight, or endorsement on General Grant at the beginning when their own General Longstreet remarked, 'I know Grant very well as a friend, and under no circumstances underestimate him or dismiss him.' General Longstreet had been right, Grant was mustering an army of over a hundred thousand men and pulling in every available resource to deliver a massive knockout punch to General Lee's Army of Northern Virginia. The punch when it came had dissolved into a series of desperate looping swings that had stunned Lee's army, but had not quite destroyed it. It had cost Grants army over two thousand men a day for a month, a month of solid fighting on the back foot for Lee. Lee had finally been cornered in front of Petersburg after this terrible dance of death with Grant. Still threatening, still inflicting and taking horrible casualties in trenches, in forts and in winding rifle pits.

Grant had been at Lee's throat like a frenzied terrier for six weeks, and nobody had thought on either side that it could get any worse after Gettysburg.

It had got worse, far worse, and Lee for once had been briefly duped by Grant when Grant funnelled his entire army over river crossings into a soldiers worse nightmare called the Wilderness. The Wilderness was a vast expanse of second growth trees and dense thickets, riddled with deep ravines, masked by thick bushes. A man had to cut through a tangle of brambles and creepers just to make a few yards. It was the last place on earth that a General would try to manoeuvre a gigantic army, complete with artillery and cavalry. But Grant's plan had been to jump Lee by surprise and force him into a stand up battle in the open, which could only end in defeat for Lee's army of only around sixty thousand. It might of worked as Grant's Officers guided their men onto the only road that cut through the centre of the fourteen mile long and six mile wide tangle. But Lee had soon realised what was happening and he had ploughed his entire army straight into the Wilderness to hammer Grant before he could get his far superior artillery through. This is where the General's horse had been blown clean from underneath him, and Wayne remembered the unfortunate incident as clearly as yesterday and would sometimes ponder it amongst others as he lay on his bunk at night.

It had been the Generals final battle and everybody who survived it could not believe how the old man had not been killed outright. Wayne's division had been one of the first to collide into union soldiers as they groped their way through a tangle of underbrush and saplings. The union boys had been taken by surprise and had frantically tried to fall into some semblance of a battle formation. But the battle worn rebels had quickly taken the initiative and swept forward firing and reloading their muskets as fast as possible. More Federals had come bursting through the trees and shouts of – 'See you in hell Johnnie reb and see you in hell Billy yank' – began to be drowned out by the roar of massed musketry. The scene had soon become an inferno of blazing muskets, smoke and the sickening stab of bayonets into taut flesh. Wayne was firing and reloading his musket like a demon, and was wondering if they had careered into a whole union corps.

Unfortunately they had, and were beginning to clasp hands in the dark to take the first fumbling steps in the dance of death. Nobody knew what had actually happened until long afterwards, because everybody from General down to private was fighting blind.

Union General George Getty had virtually crashed into Confederate General A.P. Hill in the dark woods, taking both of them by surprise. As they began to swap desperate punches, the famous General Hancock had quickly brought his corps up to support Getty who was outnumbered and being pushed back. Wayne's corps had hit Hancock's massed right flank, who were turning towards them and putting up a deadly fire.

The boom of field cannon joined the fray and shot and canister began to split and fell trees all around the terrified soldiers. All around, Wayne's comrades were being shot and decapitated and his stomach was churning over with fear and nausea. They were being beaten badly now and outnumbered two to one, as they tried to rally.

Suddenly the General had burst onto the scene, leading a batch of reserve troops. He was astride his horse, galloping around waving his hat like a demented rodeo showman.

Through the flames, smoke and thunderous noise, two separate battle lines began to take shape, blazing away at each other without let-up. Wayne could feel himself being caressed either side by the welcome shoulders of his comrades. Then, without warning the ugly nose of an artillery piece protruded from between two trees and blew the General's horse clean from underneath him, ripping a hole in the ranks behind him. Wayne had looked on in amazement, as the General appeared to hang in mid air for a few seconds, then drop heavily onto his feet in the underbrush. He staggered around as if he was doing a peculiar bow-legged barn dance, then slumped against a tree and slowly slid down, falling prostrate. Everybody thought that he must be dead from the sheer impact, but incredibly the old man rolled over and tried to stand up.

Now it became a desperate lunge to try to rescue the General and deny the Federals of their prize. A few boys ran forward and were promptly cut down as if they had been swiped by a scythe.

From behind Wayne, boys were coming in and around returning a deadly fire, which was ripping into the massed Federals, cutting them to smithereens. But the weight of numbers was too great and Wayne began to feel the cold caress of being flanked from both sides, as the Federals began to envelop them.

Suddenly the musketry burst into an ear bursting crescendo and Wayne felt that the jaws of death were about to bite him. Then as if by some miracle the Union musketry turned slowly to its own left flank and the unmistakable sound of the rebel yell came sweeping through the trees like a furious banshee. General Longstreet had arrived with his hard fighting Texan brigade and the odds were suddenly evened out.

Now it was the Federals turn to be pushed back or flanked, and Wayne, covered with the others, so that a couple of boys could run forward and pull the grateful General to safety. All the old man could say was, 'Thanks boys, just keep after em…'

The boys had a great deal of affection for the General and when he was replaced by a younger man, who the high command in all their wisdom thought may bring something new and innovative to the war, the boys had been bitterly disappointed.

Major General Clegg who replaced him was indeed gallant, brave and daring, but sadly he had been killed by a sharpshooter at Cold Harbor. His replacement had found himself trying to patch up a fraying and hole ridden division whose dead veterans simply could not be replaced. But by this time Wayne had finally been caught by a red-hot musket ball in front of Spotsylvania courthouse.

This was another episode that haunted him as he lay on his bunk at night. Even worse it would appear as a nightmare, intermingled with countless other shadowy dreams and wrench him screaming from his sleep. He could remember every detail and feel every event, because it was constantly with him, cajoling and snapping at him mercilessly.

He had been well within his own lines helping to move twenty-six field pieces from the horseshoe, which was soon to become the bloody angle.

General Lee had suspected an attack somewhere else and had thought it safe enough to take away these pieces, as the lines that met at this point at right angles were so heavily fortified that it would be sheer suicide to try and carry them. But this is precisely where the mysterious General Grant had planned to strike, in force.

The dawn was breaking and a fine drizzle had began to fall as Wayne looked down from the heights onto the diverging lines. The sloping ground with an abatis craftily placed at different points to impede any line of attack would indeed be extremely difficult to attack successfully. Thankfully for the Confederates they had managed to beat the Federals to this crucial point that was the main turnpike down to Richmond.

It had been a desperate race, and when the two armies had fought two days and nights to a standstill; turning a full semi-circle in the first steps of the dance in the murky Wilderness woods, both Generals wondered what the other one would do next.

Grant had been the first to move. He had mustered his Generals in the night and orders were given to put their battered brigades on the road, and this time they were moving south. When Lee had got wind of the move, he quickly gave orders to head him off, at all costs. This had come across as a bad surprise to the boys, because every union General before had moved their shattered armies north, after clashing with the monolithic Lee. Thankfully a massive fisticuffs between two rival union cavalry corps, which lasted a full two hours gave Lee enough time to get the edge on Grant.

When they had finally got their troops in place Wayne found himself digging in with all of the rest, frantically building fieldworks; working through sheer exhaustion. Another stand up fight was inevitable and stout, impregnable fortifications would be the only way to repel the onslaught. The onslaught would come rapidly, in blind fury.

The first snapping sounds of picket line fire had caught Wayne's attention, but had not unduly alarmed him. As the sound became more frequent and heavy, Wayne had begun to wonder if a decoy attack was being made on the horseshoe, to force Lee to reinforce it, while the main attack was conducted somewhere else along the lines.

But his adrenaline began to churn around in his stomach, as the familiar sound of massed musketry began to herald the arrival of a main attack coming their way. The Colonel had been looking down on the scene, trying to see what was going on through drizzle through his binoculars. Finally he slipped his binoculars back into their pouch and his words would haunt Wayne forever.

"Right boys, load your muskets before moving down. We're in for a hellova' fight."

Automatically Wayne slipped into place of the double line battle formation. His usual place on the extreme left flank of the front line. He could remember each barked order, every clear word, as he had a thousand times before. - 'Right boys, load muskets, front rank open up six feet apart, to give clear line of fire to the rear rank. Forward march' -

As they slowly swept down from the heights Wayne could hear the familiar tune of, 'The Campbell's Are Coming' - coming from the far off left flank of the union lines and he immediately knew that would be the actual decoy attack. He was right, as they came into the rear of the horseshoe the boys in front were laying on a heavy fire from all angles, trying to avoid the panic stricken rebel pickets who were being pursued back to their own lines. Daylight had began to creep across the fields and Wayne could see the faded blue uniforms of the union boys, bobbing and weaving, loading and firing, ducking and diving. They were being cut to shreds, before getting within a hundred yards of the horseshoe. Bodies were already piling up, between and on every bristling abatis and spiked fence. Wayne vaguely thought to himself that this was pure unadulterated murder. But still the Federals came charging forward, battle flags waving resolutely. Wayne knew by the way they were zig-zagging and dropping to the ground to dodge the salvos, they were facing Potomac veterans, possibly Sedgwick's, Warrens or Hancock's boys. Some of the rebel boys began to gasp in horror, because the attack was being pressed home despite the causalities and futility of it.

Wayne could see loaded muskets being passed up to the boys on the defences, then being fired and handed back and other ones being passed up in quick succession.

Occasionally a boy would drop from the defences, with blood pouring from his face or head. But this was a one sided fight and Wayne was thinking that surely they cannot carry on, but they did. The Colonel had ordered them to stay forty yards back from the nose of the horseshoe, just in case it was breached. More boys began to drop from the defences all around and were quickly replaced. By now the sloping ground before the horseshoe was littered with the dead and wounded, and still they kept coming, piling in from behind. Now the faded blue uniforms were gone and boys in crisp new blue regalia came marching in, in perfect drill formation. These were unfortunate artillery boys who had been drafted into the infantry and had no idea of how the old infantry had long thrown away this line of attack. As they came into the open, shoulder to shoulder they were like sitting ducks. They did not have enough time to release even one effective salvo before being cut down by blazing, concentrated musket fire.

By now some of the detached artillery pieces had been brought back onto the horseshoe and the result they had as they let rip with canister and shot was devastating. Wayne was glancing around, taking stock of the expressions on the other boys' faces and they were silently reflecting his own thoughts; surely they cannot carry on.

Unbelievably the union boys were clambering and climbing over piled up bodies that were disintegrating and falling apart with shot. The blue wave kept rolling forward and suddenly they were pouring into the first lines of trenches. Frenzied stabbing and clubbing ensued and the boys up on the defences were given orders to fix bayonets. The Colonel quickly followed suit, – 'Right boys fix bayonets and stand by.' – The bloodthirsty brawl grew, then began to finally roll up onto the defences. The terrible cry of the desperate and dying rose as the stabbing and point blank musket fire desecrated tortured body and soul. Wayne watched in stunned silence as the union boys began to sweep up towards them. The Colonel waited until they were about twenty yards away and then shouted, – 'FIRE' – The first wave was instantly shattered, leaving only a few who staggered forward, that were soon dispatched by bayonet and sword. The second wave swept forward and the boys in the rear fired off their salvos, with the same result.

Now from either flank the rebels that were positioned in higher redoubts began firing down onto the Federal assault, which was now being crushed by its own massed reinforcements. Wayne's lines were busy working their ramrods and inflicting as much damage as possible with their red-hot muskets. But the wave of blue clad boys was coming over so thick and fast that they had to be overrun. Wayne could hear movement from behind and gratefully knew that they were being backed up rapidly.

Then without warning the shouts of, LEE! LEE! LEE! Came sweeping down from behind and a strange calm came over

Wayne and he could sense that the rest of the boys could feel it. Now the old man was in charge, his presence could be clearly felt. But could he pull them out of this one, this time? The Colonel could obviously feel it too, because he casually moved to the front, lifted his sword and roared the words – 'CHARGE.' – Wayne's line ran down to engage the enemy, who were firing straight at them. To the left and right of him boys were being shot dead on their feet as they ran, dropping heavily in the blood soaked mud. Wayne was one of the first to clash with the union boys, plunging his bayonet deep into the chest of a bearded, bear-like man. He felt sick and nauseated with every fibre of his being as he watched the man's eyes flicker and die. He pulled the bayonet free and thrust it savagely into the side of a tall, slim youth who was grappling with one of the boys. The youth who was probably a placid clerk or store worker in his former life, groaned in agony and toppled forward, dying in horrible pain. The rear rank rushed into the fray, firing, impaling and swinging their muskets like clubs. But the Federals were putting up a furious fight and were firing and stabbing at them with uncontrollable aggression. The defences had now been breached in several places and blue clad soldiers were swarming around islands of grey clad ones on and around the defences. The Colonel ordered the remainder of them to pull back, as the position could not be held. This is when Wayne felt his musket butt jar sharply in his hands as a musket ball struck it, then a sharp pain in his thigh as it rebounded straight down into his leg. He fell forward and slid around in the mud, before falling face down.

He rolled over onto his back and watched in despair as the boys pulled back, still firing. One of them tried to pull him up by his arm, but fell backwards as a hail of musket fire swept up the slope, like tiny messengers of sudden pain and death. He could see the union boys moving forward and suddenly they were all about him, firing and cursing with demented anger at their tormentors and the faceless demons of war who had put them there. Wayne was now being trampled into the mud as the union boys moved up the slope in block. Once again he could hear the chant of, LEE! LEE! LEE! And a deafening barrage of musket fire and roar of cannon fire came flying back down. Decapitated bodies flew into the air and the groans of the dying sounded like a distant lonely lament. Still the union boys tried to press on and the bodies piled up all around and on top of Wayne until he felt that he was suffocating with the sheer weight. He could feel their warm blood soaking his hair and clothing, then running down his chest. He could smell their musky, sweat stained clothing, which seemed to imply to him, 'we smell and bleed just like you Johnnie reb.' Then he slowly slipped into oblivion with the distant chant of, LEE! LEE! LEE! Still accompanying him.

He had woken up the next day in a field hospital, his right leg swathed in bandages. In the next bed to his, an old timer had been watching him intently as he came round, his own head covered in bloody bandages. Wayne clearly remembered his words.

"Welcome back to the land of the living boy, remember what happened to yah."

Vaguely, Yankee bullet caught me in the leg," Wayne had replied.

"Watched them pull yah out after we knocked 'em back, for getting hit meself."

"Can remember being in one hellova fight, but don't know what happened."

"Yah boys did real good, stopped the Federals in their tracks with that bayonet charge… Gave us nuff time tah rally, put another line of defence at back, for sending help to yah… How many was there in yah company?" asked the old timer, while leaning over.

"Four hundred and twenty at the last count," said Wayne.

"Wow, heard yah lost hundred and seventy boys… There're talk 'bout the rest of yah's being merged into three corps and five corps. Damned injustice, your boys deserve better." Even the old man asked what corps was that down there fighting like wildcats. "Ha, ha, ha, some of the boys had to pull him off his horse and drag him to the rear to stop him riding down. Ha, ha, ha, big, strong fella for an old un, took four boys built like barns to carry him off, kickin, and bucking like a damn mule."

Wayne could still hear the chants of, LEE! LEE! Ringing around inside his head. The old timer leaned further over towards Wayne and began to speak more seriously.

"Mah buddy tells me that he's hearin from some of the Federal prisoners that they are angry at there own command 'bout the attack… Rumours flyin' 'bout they lost over seven thousand boys in the first half-hour round the horseshoe alone. Over twelve thousand in all, with the other assaults along the line, worse than us at Gettysburg…"

"How many did we lose…?" asked Wayne.

"Think 'bout two or three thousand, not sure yet, I'll ask mah Buddy."

The old timers estimate about the casualties had been quite accurate and most of Wayne's company became merged into five corps who had also sustained heavy losses.

Wayne had plenty of time on his hands now, to think, remember and digest all that had happened to him in four terrible, lonely years. Loneliness to Wayne was nothing new. He had always been a loner by nature, preferring the company of his beautiful beasts, than that of the complicated and irrational ways of his fellow man. It was not that he disliked or distrusted his fellow man, it was just the way he had been born. The only person he had actually disliked in his life was his older brother, Wyatt. But now Wyatt was dead, he was killed at Shiloh and Wayne had deeply regretted not getting to know his bookish, gawky brother who hated working on the farm with a vengeance.

Then, three months before war finally broke out when General Beauregard fired on Fort Sumter, Wayne's opinion of Wyatt had changed dramatically. Wyatt had changed from a sheepish bookworm to a fantastic, mysterious character to Wayne. It was the only thing that could bring bitter tears to his eyes as he lay on his bunk at night. He would turn it over and over in his mind – Why had he not tried to get to know Wyatt better? What on earth had inspired him to do the most audacious, daring, suicidal and foolish folly, was completely beyond Wayne's comprehension. Why? Why? Why?

Of all the unlikely people to hoodwink and humiliate the tyrannical and terrifying Ben Boucher, the biggest plantation owner in the county, it had been Wyatt, meek, mild Wyatt. And Wayne had thanked God everyday afterwards that he had been the only one to know. Even Wyatt did not know that Wayne knew. And if he had been found out, it would have been certain disaster for the whole family. When the news had erupted like a wrathful thunderstorm, every man in the town, from big, brawny plantation hand, to storekeeper had trembled in their boots. Everybody knew about old man Boucher's temper, even over the most trivial slight. But whoever had done this outrage against him, must have been either mad or willing to be horsewhipped to death for something they vehemently believed in. As brothers they could not have been more different. Wayne had inherited his father's Irish good looks. Thick, corn blond hair, sky blue eyes and five feet ten powerful frame. But before him came Wyatt. Oh Wyatt.

Before the war life had been good for Wayne. From a young age he had fallen into work around his father's smallholding quite naturally and his father had coaxed and nurtured his obvious love for horses. They had never been rich, but the little corn, potatoes and cotton they grew in there compact but fertile fields had tided them over quite well. Pat Rawlins had always had a strong inclination to keep horses and to sell them, and his stables had become somewhat of a sideline. He would also buy horses that were brought to him by a mysterious and frugal old timer named Bill Harding.

Harding would ride onto the ranch some afternoons after weeks of tracking wild horses in the wild and let Pat take a look at them.

Wayne could remember that these meetings had always been cordial and after Pat had chosen the ones that he wanted, he would pay Harding for them and they would chat for a while. Wayne would eavesdrop on their conversations and would become intrigued and enchanted by Bill Harding's stories.

Harding had become Wayne's first hero, and in his young boy's adventurous mind he wanted to become just like him, living wild and free. Of course the hardship and sometimes-fruitless expeditions had not really occurred to Wayne at the age of ten. But the seed of an innermost desire had been planted and quite unintentionally watered.

Then when Wayne had turned sixteen Harding's visits had become less frequent, because of old age and not being able to keep up with his rough life. But he would still visit once or twice a year and as Wayne passed his eighteenth birthday, he had told Pat a story that would haunt Wayne like a mysterious dream. It was another episode in his pre war life that he would recall fondly, wishing he could recapture it with longing.

Harding had told Pat that for the past couple of years he had being tracking a wild bunch of the most magnificent horses that he had ever seen, possibly about a hundred or so. Tracking was as far as he had got, because every time he had got close they had escaped, or rather vanished. Harding had never believed the old Indian legend about the region; regarding a wild bunch of horses that would lead anybody that could actually keep in contact with them to their happy hunting ground. Harding was an old stalwart and pragmatist, who had never had any time for such fancies. All he could tell Pat was that the whole area above and between the Mississippi and Yazoo rivers, above Vicksburg was prone to flooding and a devil of a place to track horses. And definitely not a place to stay for a long time without adequate supplies. His last odyssey had been his hardest and by far the worst. He had been tracking them day and night after he had finally caught sight of them after weeks of searching. He had been moving through driving rain and fording invisible streams due to heavy flooding, sometimes floundering around with the head of his horse barely above water.

Sometimes he would have to sleep in a hammock tied between two trees, because there had been no dry land in sight.

He had finally lost track of them completely up near the Yalobusha River, close to some high ground and a large outcrop of tall, sheer rocks. This was ground, which the indigenous Indian regarded as sacred and forbidden. Harding had confessed that he had camped close by to them all night and in the morning they had just vanished without trace. But by this time he had been too exhausted and delirious with dysentery to carry on looking for them. Wayne knew that his father had trusted Harding, and when it became apparent that he could not clear this particular story from his head, he told Pat of his wishes. His only escape and refuge from the terrible thoughts, dreams and pain of the past four years had been to reflect on this period, three years before war was declared. And he would savour this in the early hours, just before dawn.

CHAPTER 3

Whispers of a delta breeze. May 1858.

It had been plaguing and nagging at him all day, as it had done for weeks, and as Wayne crossed the yard, sat in the porch and kicked off his boots, he could not hold it back any longer. He had to do it and get this bug out of his system.

"Pa… The old yarn that Harding used to tell 'bout that elusive herd o hosses down over the delta… Well, doyah believe it? I mean he never caught one as proof."

Pat, who was leaning on the porch, smoking his pipe and gazing out over to the distant mountains quietly pondered Wayne's words and eventually answered.

"Well son, ole' Harding never sold me a bad hoss in over twenty years. Can't say that I understand the old bull, but he ain't the kinda dude that frequents saloons and brags 'bout his business… Yeh son, bleeve must be some truth in it, some truth."

"Well Pa, been workin' hard all week, got most of the jobs outa the way… nough hay and water for the hosses for ten or twelve days… Been thinkin' for some time to go and take a look for maself… Pa, I just can't git this outa ma head, don't understand it…"

Pat looked down towards him smiling wryly and blew out a cloud of blue smoke.

"I know son, I know somethins' bin on yah mind for some time. Had a hunch it might of bin that. Coz I was watchin' yah face all those years ago when Harding told the story. If I was young agin and didn't have to care for yah Ma, I would probably wanna go and look for 'em maself. I would wanna' come with yah as well, but yah know I can't son."

Mary Rawlins who had been standing in the doorway unnoticed by them both said, "Wayne, the ideas yah get in that head o yours, ole Harding is a dreamer with no responsibilities or ties. Yah shouldn't o listened to him too much."

They both turned to face Mary, whose face was yellow and drawn, indicating the final stages of tuberculosis and typhoid and Pat spoke first.

"Let him go Mary, I can take care things round here for a couple o weeks, besides I've always been interested in that particular yarn maself, I even told yah, years ago."

"Pity yah's don't wanna study like Wyatt, Wayne, he's gonna be a teacher one day and leave all this farm life in his past, can't blame him for that," said Mary, almost piously.

This was a real sore point with Wayne, and Mary had quite unwittingly touched his most sensitive nerve. He snapped at her angrily, with saliva bursting from his mouth.

"What would Wyatt know about farm life Ma, he's never lifted a pitchfork, ploughed a field, planted corn, reaped a harvest, broke a hoss, nothin', nothin', I spose you'd rather see me sittin' with him ree-citen' poetry with Tom Boucher like some damn fool fancy dude. Ma, me and Wyatt just ain't the same, can't you understand that…?"

Pat interrupted and spoke in his customary calm, collective manner.

"I said he can go Mary, the boy needs a change, to do something different."

Mary had the unfortunate trait that some mothers have, of being completely oblivious to what can only be perceived as favouritism by anybody else, made matters worse.

"Wayne, I only want the best for both of you… By the way, I almost forgot. I saw Mary Lou in town today, she was askin' 'bout yah Wayne. Fine, fine family. Do so much for the community, good God fearing Christians, never miss a church service. Mary Lou would sure make a fine bride and daughter in-law."

By this time Wayne almost had steam blowing out of his ears. He was everything but what his mother thought he should be. Mary Lou was indeed a fine gal. So was Jesse Jo, so was Liz Cockburn, so were many other eligible gals in town. They sure did look fine in the white frocks and Sunday bonnets. But Wayne was simply not interested.

Just as Wayne had begun to calm down, across the yard a shed door opened, or rather Wyatt's study door. Wyatt emerged, adjusted his sight to the daylight, put his glasses on and walked towards them. His spindly legs, matchstick thin arms and painfully thin body made it look as though it was a task just for him to walk upright. From somewhere long back in the gene pools of his Irish forefathers and his German foremothers came Wyatt. Wayne, who had inherited everything from his father, other than patience and tolerance for somebody he deemed to be a damned fool remarked, "Well, well. He would sure make a damn fine scarecrow, if nothin' else."

"Easy Wayne, yah Ma don't need any more arguments now," said Pat.

"Okay Pa, I don't wanna cause any trouble, but I can't stand the worthless cuss."

With that he stood up and walked into the house, still grumbling and fuming.

Two days later, in the early hours, Wayne mounted his favourite horse Long Horn and nudged the magnificent black beast into a canter. The sun had begun to peep over the distant mountains, like a red, benevolent eye. It felt good to be alive as the horse gently kicked up dust and expertly accommodated its powerful, yet tender master.

Both Pat and Wayne knew that it was the best solution for him to get away from the farm for a while. They all knew Mary was dying, but Wayne's understandable bad feelings towards Wyatt had reached boiling point. When Wayne had been sarcastic to the equally bookish and gawky Tom Boucher, the second son of the infamous Ben, Pat knew his son was becoming dangerously flippant. Wayne had thrown a stone through the window of Wyatt's study when Wyatt and Tom Boucher were reciting poetry aloud and it had narrowly missed Tom's head. Wayne actually preferred Tom's older brother, John, who was in the same mould as his brutal, intolerant father. This was despite hearing awful tales of cruelty to the Boucher slaves by John from Wade Cockburn, who worked for them. Wayne believed Wade, because he knew John from his aloof and cold manner. And he knew that Wade only worked for the Boucher's because extreme family poverty forced him to. Now Wayne was gratefully escaping from everything.

Two days later he was overlooking the Yazoo and Mississippi Delta from the heights of Chickasaw Bluffs, surveying the same panoramic view as Bill Harding had done so many times before. He crossed the Yazoo River just north of the bluffs late in the afternoon and camped under a cluster of low slung pine trees.

As he lit a fire and boiled coffee he realised that this was his true vocation, away from the complications and realities of society. The noise of grasshoppers, crickets and chirping of the delta birds was like music to his ears. As the sun went down and the wind began to whisper through the trees and across the lush and long delta grass and reeds, Wayne wondered at the beauty of it all and was overcome by a deep feeling of peace and tranquillity.

His sleep had come in two and three-hour periods, the strange noises of the delta had disturbed him. Noises, which made him wonder what strange creatures of the night they belonged to. And as dawn broke and he stashed his blankets and pots away, the mixed feelings of anticipation and adventure overwhelmed him. The lush grass and abundant stretches of shallow water due to an abnormally rainy season, meant that Long Horn could graze and drink at his own leisure. And as Wayne saddled him and stroked his shiny black mane, he said as if he was confiding in him, "Well Long, let's see if we can find this band of ghost horses."

They were completely alone in the wild, with only the whispers of a delta breeze.

Riding on the wind.

Wayne had spent the next four days wandering around the areas of Sunflower River, Deer creek and Rolling fork. During this time it had slowly dawned on him that to search for horses, in particular horses whose whereabouts were far from certain, was a painstaking and difficult task.

His sojourn had been completely fruitless. Not even the scent or sign of a single horse had manifested itself. Now this was the first time he had begun to realise that to live like Harding was a long and lonely vigil, with no sure-fire booty at the end of the road. To add to his problems, some of the stretches of flooded plains had been deceptively deep in places and he had been forced to make long, round detours just to gain a few miles. Finally he had decided to move northwards, between Sunflower River and deer Creek. He had also discovered that insects and bugs may be pleasing to the ear, but they can also bite and inflict infuriating irritations, even under clothing. As he moved north into country riddled with winding, overgrown rivulets, that had only ever been graced by presence of the rare Indian hunter, he began to wonder if he had made a mistake.

It had been his eleventh night in the wild. His enthusiasm had dwindled dramatically as he lashed up and stowed his gear. He had been pondering the thoughts of holding out for another day or two and then heading home. He was no defeatist, but horses normally left some sign or indication that they had visited or wandered in an area. There had been nothing whatsoever to give him a line of further investigation, besides, he was becoming extremely uncomfortable.

Then, as he forded yet another muddy stream, to cross the expanse of another watery plain that stretched to infinity he pulled Long Horn to a sudden halt. In the distance he could see what he thought was a moving rainbow on the glass-like water. It was horses. A lot of horses, moving at speed and casting up cascades of spray as they ran. He could not hide his sheer delight as he shouted gleefully to Long Horn.

"Harding was telling the truth, they're real, real as you and me. Let's git after 'em!"

He dug his heels sharply into Long Horn's ribs and pulled his reins to guide him towards the rapidly rolling rainbow. The horse responded perfectly and once they had cleared some clumps and clods of growth they were away, gliding through the shallow water at speed.

The wind caught Wayne's thick blond hair and the excitement of the chase rocketed up from his solar-plexus, like fire. But this band of phantom horses were moving away at incredible speed, fuelling Wayne's spirit, with wild abandon.

"Yah won't git away from me like yah did ole Harding!" he shouted and laughed.

But to his amazement, they were getting away, rolling away through a cascading, dancing rainbow. He kicked his heels as hard as he dared into Long Horn and the powerful streamline horse thundered into a long spanning gallop. Wayne had never handled a horse as fast and strong as Long Horn and he could not believe that any horse could out run him over a long stretch. But these beauties were, and there were at least a hundred of them. Then quite suddenly Wayne could see that the ground rose up from the water, into a long slanting gradient, decked sparsely with pines and solitary oaks.

The rainbow vanished into thin air as they panned out from the water, onto the high ground and now he could see them clearly. Blacks. Browns. Whites, and mixed colourings of the biggest and most beautiful beasts that he had ever seen.

"Come on Long Horn boy, come on, they can't keep this pace up...!" he yelled. But they could and were, the rising ground had not stifled there pace at all, it had only spread them out. And still they kept moving, darting and probing like a rising tide. As steed and master cleared the final stretch of water that had now begun to ripple on a sweeping downwind, Wayne wondered if Long Horn could carry on at this pace for much longer. But the horse could feel and breath the heart and soul of his master and as they rode up onto the high ground the noble, gracious beast found his second wind.

Wayne's eyes were watering from the gushing wind and he had to blink consistently to drain the tears down his cheeks. But he never took his eyes away from the host speeding before him. The ground gradually began to even out and slant downwards and Wayne found he was now guiding Long Horn downwards to another water plain.

Gratefully Wayne observed that the host had slowed down as they approached the shimmering water. And by the time they had glided into the shallow lake, most of them had slowed down to a canter. Wayne breathed a deep sigh of relief.

"Oh Long Horn, it looks like they're in home territory, now we just gotta keep a distance and follow 'em... Well done boy, well done. I knew I could rely on yah."

Wayne had never known a family of horses that were so sensitive to unfamiliar noise, so aware of each others presence, and very fast to react to even one or two of them being alarmed. They also knew each other implicitly. Wayne had been following them at a safe distance for two days and nights. Tiredness had only become a slight inconvenience for him, because sheer excitement had completely engulfed his emotions. How he would catch even one of them was another question. But over the past two days he had contemplated this question from another position. Did he really want to catch even one, or just find out where they went and ultimately vanish as Indian legend and the dogmatic Harding professed. He had camped as close as he dared when they had stopped to graze and settle for the night, using clusters of bunched trees and bushes as cover. Sleep had only come in uncomfortable and staggered bouts, because he did not want them to slip away quietly as he slept.

After another two days of careful tracking, the land had become a lot more overgrown and tangled, with saplings and gorse bushes slashing Long Horn's legs. Wayne thought that this was the ultimate no mans land, where only wild animals could live by brook and stream, safe from man. The horses knew the lay of the land well, and led Wayne even through the densest areas quite easily, while he deftly followed them.

Then, as they entered onto a grassy plain Wayne was struck by the sight of a large outcrop of rocks, tall and sheer clustered in the centre of the plain. This is where Harding must have lost them, all those years ago.

The grass here was lush and an odd Lincoln green in colour, and the horses stopped and hungrily devoured it. Wayne remembered what Harding had told him and thought that it would be nigh on impossible to escape a seasoned old tracker like Harding from this prime position. But as it became apparent that the horses intended to stay here for the night, Wayne had an instinct that he would have to watch their every move. There was a mysterious chill in the air.

Wayne's gut feeling had been right, because in the early hours, just as dawn was breaking, a magnificent black stallion began to canter in a large anti clockwise circle. Wayne watched in amazement as all of the rest of them began to follow suit, until they were all moving together in perfect harmony. He became galvanised and filled with awe, as he had never seen anything like this before. Then quite suddenly, the stallion that had instigated this strange dance peeled away from them and started slowly moving towards the rocks. The rest followed in single file, keeping at exactly the same pace and distance between each other. Wayne began to follow the last one, staying as close as he dared. They began to weave through the rocks, some of which were gigantic. Some looked like tall, black tombstones planted by an invisible giant hand.

Wayne had not seen any rocks like this in the area, they appeared completely foreign to the terrain, as if they had been dropped from the sky. The centrepiece was a hundred feet high twin spire, which looked like twin stone barrels rammed together and bulging at the base. As the horses moved towards the base, weaving through boulders and sheer rock faces, the ground dropped sharply. From his position Wayne could see that the peculiar looking centrepiece was surrounded by a natural and very deep moat, giving the impression of an impregnable castle. The moat was at least fifty yards wide and as the line of horses headed down towards it, Wayne thought that they were going to quench their thirsts, but he became electrified as the leading stallion dithered for a while and then began to walk into the water. Surely it must be far too deep and sheer to bathe in, but the horse floundered for a while and then its hooves found solid ground.

The beast appeared to be concentrating on what it was doing now, as it slowly moved out at a right angle towards the face of the rock. Then slowly, in single file the rest followed him in exactly the same manner, without wavering. Wayne predicted that they were following a sunken causeway that nearly covered their shoulders, but where were they heading for? He could clearly see the tide mark at the base of the rock, which was at least six feet above the present water line. This meant that in the rainy season the causeway would be at least ten feet under water. Then the leading horse began to climb the rock face on some jagged steps that could not be seen from the shore. Suddenly it appeared to vanish into the rock face, about twenty feet up the side. Wayne blinked his eyes and watched the rest follow. It took him some time to adjust his sight and when he did he realised that they were entering a small dark fissure, that could just about accommodate a big horse. It looked no different from any of the outer fissures, or pockmarks that decked the rock face, and was perfectly camouflaged.

Wayne knew in his heart that this must be the source of the story from Indian legend. And if this place was deemed sacred and out of bounds to the ancient Indians, then he was probably the only human being who had ever witnessed this. He could not turn back now, he must find out where they had gone.

"Come on Long Horn, let's see if we can follow 'em," he said quietly.

Long Horn's initial steps into the water were very timid, and Wayne could sense that the horse was afraid. But the animal's love for its master overcame its fear and gradually after some delicate foot finding, its hooves found the pebbles of the causeway. Wayne carefully guided his trusted horse by gently tugging on the reins either side. The adrenaline began to churn around in his stomach as he realised that the causeway was very narrow and dropped sharply into deep water on both sides. Finally after what seemed like an eternity Long Horn began to rise out of the water and cautiously climb the sheer, narrow steps. Wayne had to duck low as he coaxed the horse into the blackness of the fissure.

He put a match to a torch, which he had taken from his saddlebag. About twenty yards inwards the fissure spanned out into a dome-like cave and at the end of the cave he could see daylight. He aimed Long Horn towards the daylight and noticed that it emanated from another narrow fissure.

As he passed through the fissure into the daylight, he could not believe his eyes. All around him there was greenery, trees and coloured flowers of which he had never seen before. He was standing on the edge of what could be interpreted as the Garden of Eden. By some freak of nature the twin rocks had become like an enormous flowerpot, enclosing black fertile soil and watering it with small waterfalls that cascaded down the sides of the sheer walls. In one corner was a deep blue lake of pure mountain water that was naturally serviced by underground caves that drained and changed the water, so it never flooded. He could see that the horses were prancing around in the shallows.

They had come home, probably as they had done for countless generations, after long expeditions of foraging. Come back to perhaps two acres of paradise, completely protected by the wind. Various birds nested in the sheer walls, occasionally leaving their nests and soaring up and over the heights. This explained the marked contrast in trees and fauna. Huge oaks and maples, shaded violets, poppies and daffodils, the seeds from all of this plant life brought in and dropped in the dung of birds that had migrated to and from far off lands. There were cuttings and caves at the base of the walls, providing perfect shelter for a lot of horses. The same type of deep green grass that circled the parameters of the citadel was here in abundance. The minerals from rock and water feeding and colouring it through the black, fertile soil. Sunbeams had begun to penetrate downwards and sweep over everything. The blue of the water, green of the trees, the warm caress of the sun and sound of cascading water overwhelmed Wayne's senses. A deep peace came over him, and he wished that he could share it, share it with somebody, although he did not know whom.

He would never recapture this sense of peace again for a long time, because the seeds of another kind were slowly being scattered and sown. And they would burst forth in less than three years down the line. They were the seeds of war and they would not spring in colour and morning dew. They would sprout in blood, anger, and tear the hearts from thousands of innocent young men. But at this moment in time Wayne's only thoughts as he carefully negotiated the causeway and made his way back onto the delta plains were, 'did he tell anybody about what he had discovered? Or did he keep it all a secret?' He finally concluded, 'who would believe him anyway.'

Suddenly a loud distant thunderclap, followed by the burble of rolling thunder brought him back to reality. Long Horn became unusually disturbed and for some strange reason, so did Wayne. Bolts of lightning stabbed down onto the land, from black rolling clouds, warning the humid air of its stormy intent and presence. Both man and beast were familiar with the roar of thunder, it had been a frequent visitor lately, although keeping at a safe distance. Wayne gently reassured Long Horn.

"Don't fret boy, it ain't cannon fire. It can't hurt us. Easy boy, easy, easy."

It had occurred to Wayne that he used the words, 'cannon fire' when addressing his horse and wondered why. The only cannons he had ever seen were the ancient, highly polished ones that graced the big doorways of the Boucher place, as ornaments. He did not expect to see or hear such a weapon in his life, and he certainly did not want to witness what this weapon could do to the human body. But he would; he would see canister and shot rip human flesh and bone to shreds. He would see what multitudes of heavy guns could meter out, in countless battlefields. Battlefields that were at the present time sleepy hamlets and pleasant fields and turnpikes. Pleasant romantic names would turn into names of horror, blood and death, as if an ugly black shadow had swept over and desecrated them, indelibly stamping their names in the ether forever.

But for now he was a boy of nineteen, full of the hunger, wonder and soul searching anticipations of youth. And as he kicked Long Horn into a slow trot, he felt wild and free. It felt so good to be alive.

CHAPTER 4

I don't pree-fess to know.

Wayne was walking with Ty Murphy along one of the winding lanes that circled the vast expanse of the Boucher plantation, Ty towered over Wayne and his big, heavy boots were leaving deep imprints in the dusty path. Wayne had been nursing a feeling of trepidation as they rounded a sunken bend, overgrown with weeds and gorse. He did not really want to see a dead body, in particular one that had been hanged. But Ty had insisted, besides he wanted to talk to Wayne in private.

Ty said enthusiastically, "he's just round this corner. Ole Boucher won't cut him down for a few days."

"What did yah wanna talk 'bout Ty can't think of a worse time and place."

Then just as they rounded the bend Wayne saw him and gagged with horror. The young black slave was hanging fifteen feet above the ground, from the branch of an ancient oak tree. The bright yellow rope that had strangled the life out of him was blatantly the insignia of Ben Boucher, like a macabre advert or veiled warning.

"Okay Ty, I've seen him and I don't like what I see... Now what...?"

"Well, what do yah notice 'bout him Wayne?"

"Well, apart from being as naked as a jaybird, he looks like he was a big strong fella."

"Come on Wayne. What else do yah notice 'bout him?"

"He's been horse whipped real badly, just look at those welts. Whoever did that to him must of done it with hatred in his heart, beyond belief."

"Come on Wayne, what else do yah notice 'bout him?"

"Well apart form his dick is nearly as big as Long Horns, he's very dead."

"Exactly, his dick, or size of it…Now I know why you call Long Horn, Long Horn."

"Your powers of dee-dution Ty, could make even Plato look like a damn fool."

"Plato? Who's Plato?"

"Some ole Greek dude my brother Wyatt is always reading 'bout."

"Do yah know why ole Boucher hanged him?" said Ty, grinning from ear to ear.

"No I don't Ty. Now will you get to the damn point Ty."

"Because of his dick, or the size of it and what he was using it for."

"What was he using it for Ty? To lasso damn hosses," said Wayne in exasperation.

Now Ty had become thoroughly delighted, because Wayne did not know why.

"Wade Cockburn works for the Boucher's, knows 'em all, includin' the three gals, Martha, Olga and Mari Jo. Well, Wade say's that Mari Jo is nothing like the other two Miss prim and Miss proper. Mari Jo is completely wild and rebellious. Apart from that crazy dude brother Tom, she hates all of 'em with a vengeance, I mean vengeeee-ance."

"Okay Ty, what's all this leadin' up to? Can see you're dyin' to tell me."

"Well Mari Jo took a likin' to this beg fella and sadused him."

"Seduced him Ty, seduced him."

"Yeh, yeh, that's what I meant. She even used Wade for excuses to take her out to the slave quarters to get her hands on him. When Wade found out he was being used by her, he shit himself. Can you imagine Boucher if he found out Wade was in on it? Even if he didn't know he was being used at the time."

"Wow, Wade must be sure glad he ain't hangin' up there next to this fella."

"He sure is, he sure is. When Wade found out the real reasons why he was ferryin' her out there in that darn crazy lookin' woman's buggy, he told her he could not keep doing it, as ole Boucher would surely think he was complissip in her subfuse."

"Complicit in her subterfuge Ty."

"Yeh, that's what I meant Wayne, that's what I meant."

Wade Cockburn was Wayne's best friend and cold sweat began to trickle down Wayne's back, as he tried to picture himself in Wade's position.

"Well how did ole Boucher find out? And how come he didn't suspect that Wade was not directly involved? I mean men like Boucher don't take no darn prisoners."

"It gets worse, it gets a lot worse," said Ty, hardly being able to conceal his delight.

"How much worse can it get Ty? I can see you're dyin' to tell me."

Ty just laughed raucously and carried on with the tale.

"Well when Wade told Mari Jo he could not carry on takin' her out to the slave quarters coz both of them were in deep trouble, she offered herself to him."

"What? What did Wade do?" asked Wayne in disbelief.

"He shat himself even more and I mean sheeee-att himself."

"My God Ty, no wonder he's lookin' so darn worried at church on Sundays, when ole Boucher gives one of his fire and brimstone sermons about the evil pleasures of the flesh. It's enough to frighten off a darn pole-cat on heat."

"Wade has got reasons to be real worried, coz when he declined Mari Jo's advances, she exposed her bosoms to him, in broad daylight."

"What? I mean, how could he resist her? She's a darn fine looking gal."

"It gets even worse Wayne, you wait for this." Now he became serious as he spoke.

"When he told her that what she was doin' was sheer madness and all three of them would surely be horsewhipped, she told him she would drag him in anyway. And worst of all, if he did not carry on ferrying her out there, she would say he tried to rape her. So he had to just keep on doin' it and hope Boucher never found out."

"How did he get outa it? He couldn't win either way," said Wayne.

"Well Boucher did find out and it worked in Wades favour. When he told me, ma darn blood ran cold Wayne, I bleeve you know somethin' 'bout John Boucher's antics."

"Wade did tell me 'bout John raping a pretty black slave gal, and when ole Boucher found out she was pregnant, he ran her off the plantation with a shot gun."

Wayne had no reason to disbelieve this, because he had witnessed Ben Boucher's uncontrollable fury before, when he had been buying a saddle and stirrups from the town's main store. Wayne had been taken completely by surprise by the events. As he was waiting to be served, Ben Boucher had burst into the store wielding a double-barrelled shotgun, foaming at the mouth and his face scarlet with rage. He had levelled the shotgun at the weird, effeminate dude who was serving a lady and fired, shattering the big mirror as the dude ducked. He then blasted the windows out, while using the most profane language and biblical oaths that Wayne had ever heard.

It turned out that this dude had been paying one of Boucher's young black male slaves for sexual favours and they had been caught in the act in one of Boucher's cotton fields by John Boucher, of all people. John had horsewhipped the boy to within an inch of his life, but the white dude had escaped. When old Boucher had found out the identity of the dude he had gone berserk. Marshall Conway and two deputies had gone out to the Boucher place to warn him about his conduct and they were also greeted by the barrels of a shotgun and some fantastic expletives. To Marshall Conway's credit he had warned Boucher that his conduct was totally unacceptable, and if he done anything like it again, he would have to run him in. Boucher had reluctantly paid for the damage, but had been completely unrepentant about his behaviour.

Ty carried on talking.

"Well when Boucher finally became suspicious, he started watching Mari Jo's every move... Luckily for Wade, she could not resist this dude and began sneakin' out to the slave quarters in the night after Wade had long gone home... He followed her out one night and caught 'em in a barn, both of 'em, stark naked, doin' it."

By now Wayne was cringing as he pictured the scene, and asked Ty cautiously, "Well, what did he do? He must of exploded like a bomb."

"He did, and that's why this poor fella had to pay, pay for both of 'em. Boucher had Mari Jo locked in her room for a few weeks and her meals only taken to her by Olga and Martha. Mari Jo ain't allowed anywhere near any male slave. Thank the Lord she never dragged Wade into it, she sure coulda done. But ole Boucher did question him."

"What did Boucher say to him? He musta been suspicious about the regular outings to the slave quarters. Only a darn fool wouldn't of suspected somethin'."

"This is where Wade played his cards very carefully, coz he knew it was a matter of life and death for him. The pregnant slave gal woz nothin' compared to what Wade told me next. And he woulda testified gains't Boucher and John to save himself. John Boucher thinks it's his divine right to abuse his father's slaves as he pleases and ole Boucher has had to even commit murder to cover John's dastardly deeds."

"Murder? Murder who?" asked Wayne.

"Another slave gal John raped and her father. Wade knows coz he helped bury the bodies. The gal's father went to the house with a knife, looking for John and ole Boucher shot him down like a dawg. Then they both murdered the gal, so she couldn't talk. Now when Boucher demanded from Wade what he knew 'bout Mari Jo and the slave, Wade did not threaten him with exposure. He simply told him this – 'I don't know Mister Boucher, I would never betray you. I mean when you and John buried that gal and her father I kept quiet, even when Marshall Conway hauled me in his office four times to learn 'bout their whereabouts and disappearance. You know I would never dare cross you Mister Boucher. I mean I've even watched the Marshall and his deputies walk right by where they're buried and never said anythin'. You know I keep quiet when I take you to see your lady friends. You know how I respect your wife.'

"Wow, what the hell else goes on up there?" said Wayne.

"Is there no damn justice Wayne? I mean, how can Boucher stand in front of a congregation and give a sermon to all those fancy ladies and dandy dudes, when his own conduct is devilish? Ain't that's what the bible calls a hypoocratt?"

"Hypocrite Ty, hypocrite."

"Will you stop contradictin' me Wayne? Yah make me sound like a darn Hill billy."

"You are a darn Hill billy Ty."

"I mean somebody, somewhere must have the guts to stop Boucher and his kind, sometime. It can't go on like this forever. What doyah think Wayne?"

"I don't pree-fess to know Ty, but I bleeve that men like ole Boucher can't change, it's the way they're made, the way they are. Even if all his cotton fields were burned to the ground, his house torched to ashes and he was being stabbed and shot to death. He could not see the errors of his ways, like a deaf, dumb and blind man. He would fight to the bitter end for what he bleeve's is his divine right."

There's talk in the north 'bout a dude called Linton, who is makin' noises 'bout stopping slavery altogether, even if it means changing the constushun."

"His name is Lincoln and I bleeve he would, if he could change the constitution. But I can't see it happening, he ain't got much support, so far."

"But what if he did get support? What doyah think would happen to Boucher and his kind, if some brave and just dude did try to stop it all?"

"I don't pree-fess to know Ty, but can't see it happenin' in our lifetimes."

"You sound like a darn Hill billy Wayne."

"I am a darn Hilly billy Ty."

CHAPTER 5

Sensual pleasures of a bodily kind.

The three of them bundled through the churchyard gate, following on the tail end of the rest of the congregation. Ty, Wade and Wayne dreaded going to church, but all three were duty bound, because to do otherwise would draw unwanted attention to their families. Wayne kicked Wade up the backside so hard, he nearly stumbled into a flock of chattering ladies dressed in their white frocks and Sunday bonnets.

Betta git going Wade, ole Boucher is gonna be givin' one of his fire and brimstone speeches today. Hate to see yah with a shotgun stuck up yah ass, if yah don't attend."

Wade shook his head of bright ginger hair as he jarred himself to a halt, narrowly missing the ladies, who looked at him in pious disdain.

"Whatyah doin' Wayne? Yah crazy bastard," he said.

This made the ladies gasp and twitter away like startled birds. Ty started laughing, Wayne's antics had been tantalising him all morning. And when Ty went into one of his laughing bouts, it was impossible for him to stop. Both Wayne and Wade knew this and deliberately played on it. It was the only way to break the boredom of this, what was to them, a ritual that they had to suffer. Wayne was in fine fettle, he simply loved goading

Wade and watching his face turn as red as his hair. From when they were young children, they had always wrestled and brawled, Wayne and Wade growing into about the same size and strength, which was very strong indeed.

As they took up their usual position at the back of the congregation they all tried to tone their horseplay down. But the appearance of the dour hawk-like priest in the pulpit made them all chortle. He looked especially dour and serious today and they would all find out why, after all the hymns were sung and all of the prayers were said.

He slammed the big black bible shut with a deliberate loud snap. This was a sure indicator that he had something very serious to say.

He twisted and distorted his face and nose and this was a certain indicator that he was really angry about something.

"Brethren, children of the faith and loyal followers of this church. Today I have something extremely important to tell you all."

He stopped talking and observed the reaction of the congregation, who went deadly quiet. What on earth could have happened in this dreary, poverty stricken town?

"For some time now, it has been brought to my attention by some good blessed folks who frequent this community, that this town has been visited by the devil himself."

The congregation all gasped together, in perfect harmony. When the priest had gauged that he had got the required reaction he went on,

"Yes, the devil himself has been creeping through this town. Not only has he been tempting some of you to indulge in sensual pleasures of a bodily kind, but a lot of you have been entertaining sensual pleasures of a bodily kind."

"Wouldn't it be simpler to say fornicating, yah damned ole fool," muttered Wayne. His words made Ty begin to snigger, and Wade nudged Wayne in the ribs.

"Don't make him laff Wayne, or we'll all be in big trouble," he whispered.

But Wayne could not resist it and as the priest continued, he began to punctuate each pause with his own lewd thoughts, and Ty had to gag from bursting into laughter.

"These bodily pleasures have ben taking place in barns, haystacks, round the back of dwellings, in fields, even in the grounds of this very church."

Again the congregation gasped on key, with unrestrained shock.

"Why do you all think I have begun to lock this holy, sacred place each night…? Because sensual pleasures of a bodily kind have been exercised in this very church."

Once again the congregation gasped in perfect harmony, which had jumped up in volume from that of a whispered prayer to an indignant, garbled burble. The distraught ladies Sunday bonnets began to bob and turn around like white ducks on agitated water.

"Yes indeed, you all have reasons to be outraged my good, God fearing flock. Yes, indeed, because in this very holy sacred place, at this very time, standing right near you are sinners, who indulge in sensual pleasures of a bodily kind."

Now the congregation did not even try to tone down their abject horror and the priest could not conceal his own gloating over this dire and dreadful news. He continued,

"The devil indeed has run amok through this once God fearing town, tempting some of you to exercise these filthy pleasures anywhere that just happens to be convenient. In fields, behind dwellings, up against walls, in this very church, anywhere..!"

By now the old priest was becoming visibly angry by his own speech and his devoted audience were fuelling his anger with sheer indignation. Ty, who was standing between Wade and Wayne, towering above them, was by now desperately trying to stop from bursting out with laughter. But Wayne would not stop adlibbing with his innuendoes.

"I sure wish I knew where these pleasures were goin' on, I could sure use some."

"Don't make him laugh Wayne, ole Boucher's up front," rasped Wade.

By this time the priest had his audience in his grasp so completely that he was manipulating them, like a maestro would do with an orchestra, by wielding a stick.

"These abominable desire's are also being exercised out of wed-lock, by fiendish fellows and lustful hussy's, who are not even satisfied with one partner."

Wayne buckled his legs slightly to hide his next comment, sensing that Ty was at exploding point with suppressed laughter.

"I would sure like to bump into some of these lustful, abominable hussy's."

Now Wade had began to snigger and blood began to rush up to his cheeks, making his face turn a dark scarlet. Wayne bent his knees lower to slip in his next remark.

"Why don't we all just have an orgy right here? We'll all sure find out who are the real bodily pleasure cowboys and gals, under their fancy clothes."

This remark had come out slightly louder than Wayne had intended and the people directly in front of them were becoming aware of the three of them. The priest was now becoming almost comic and burlesque in his pose and manner. He carried on piously,

"Oh brethren, how in the name of the good Lord are we going to purge this once beloved parish of devoted believers, of the most dastardly abomination, which the good bible deplores more than anything else? Because that revolting deed is also upon us, in barns, haystacks, cotton field and in these very grounds, lavishly."

Now Wade was having trouble fighting back laughter and his whole face was turning purple as more blood surged up into it. Wayne had noticed Wade's face and began to play on him as well as Ty. He waited patiently for the priest to finish his next tirade.

"In all the parishes I have taken the word of the good Lord to, this is by far the smallest, and by far the worst. Fornicating and sensual indulgences are not just an underlying problem, they have become a well promoted and grotesque way of life."

"Get to the point yah damned old fool, ain't anybody in this darn town got one redeemin' feature. So we're all fornicooters, proversts and feems," rasped Wade.

"Fornicators, perverts and fiends Wade. Yah don't even know what yah are."

"I know what I damn well am Wayne, just wish I could darn well do it."

Ty had to swallow hard and his face became distorted.

He pleaded with Wayne.

"Stop it Wayne, please don't carry on I can't take anymore."

But Wayne was thoroughly enjoying himself and the challenge to make Ty burst out into one of his thunderous laughs had become like a dire duty, that he must fulfil.

The congregation were now becoming aware of the sporadic horseplay and garbled comments coming from behind them and some of them had began to glance behind to see who the perpetrators were. But Wayne still could not resist goading Ty.

"Now what revolting deed are we all doing now that we don't even know about."

"It has been drawn to my attention by some of the more God fearing among you that the diabolical act of... Sod, sod, sod sodama, sodama, ma, ma, sod, soda."

Now the priest's face had become distorted and twisted, as if he was suffering constipation, or a foul taste had racked his taste buds. He could just not say the word.

"Sodomy, yah damned ole fool, sodomy, don't you read the bible," said Wayne.

Wade farted with shock, and Ty tried to mask his laugh by acting as if he had groaned in horror. But the rear-seated members of the congregation had heard Wayne's words.

"Some filthy folk are even... Sodama, sodama, ma, ma, zing, ing, sod."

"Sodomizing, yah damned old fool, sodomizing," sneered Wayne.

"It has been drawn to my attention by the good Mister Boucher that even some of his slaves have been, sod, sod, soda, ma, ma..."

"Spit it out, spit it out yah damned ole fool, let's hear it loud and clear."

"The bible itself says that the Lord will not tolerate..Sod, soda, ma, ma."

"Sodomites, sodomites...Why can't yah say it...why? Coz it don't fit into your blinkered view of the real world of sensual pleasures yah damned ole buffoon."

This had come out louder than Wayne had expected and the entire congregation turned to see who had said it, as the words echoed around the church, then slipped into deadly silence. The laugh that exploded from Ty's mouth was so loud that the whole congregation was left stupefied in shock. Then Wade's laugh also resounded around the clean white walls, his face violet with pent up hilarity at the situation. The priest was beside himself with rage and was joined by an even more furious Ben Boucher, whose face had turned a dark and dangerous purple. The priest was by now hysterical.

"Get out of my church, you heathens! Get out at once you blasphemous, filthy swine's. How dare you bring levity and lewd conduct into this sacred place? How dare you? Leave now, now. How dare you laugh at a man of the cloth?"

Ben Boucher joined in and cold fear replaced mirth as the three of them made a fast exit through the church door with Boucher's words following them out.

"How dare you laugh at the good Reverend! You heathens! How dare you?"

Wayne and Wade followed Ty as they ran along the dusty path that led away from the church and spiralled up over the hill. Ty was leaving huge footprints in the dust and his elbows were throwing apart the overgrown branches and brushwood, which were lashing back and catching Wayne and Wade. Ben Boucher's tirade could still be heard echoing around the church and bursting out through the church doors.

"How dare you bring disrespect and humiliation into the House of the Lord!"

When they had finally ran out of breath and collapsed under an old oak tree, Wade pointed at Wayne and with his face still bright red and gasping for air he said, "You've really done it this time Wayne, you've done it this time."

Only now did Wayne laugh, and that laugh echoed around the hills and mountains as wild and free as the wind.

CHAPTER 6

The man who stole a thief.

Wayne had never seen Wyatt show any emotion. In fact, anybody that knew Wyatt had ever seen him show much emotion, about anything. Even at his own mother's funeral just before the last Christmas, he had stayed in the background, cold and aloof. So what happened at their cousin's Mary Lou's wedding, shocked and stunned everybody, especially Wayne. Wayne liked Mary Lou, with her long blond hair and sweet manner. Although they had very little contact, because she lived out of town on another small, tightly run, frugally orientated small holding, owned by her parents, there had always been a congenial friendship between them. He did not know the fancy dude Lyle from Atlanta that she was marrying, but he had wished her all the best.

The drama, which had suddenly erupted after the wedding was another gut wrenching memory that Wayne would brood over, leaving him with yet another unanswered question. It would manifest itself like other pieces of a puzzle of a person that he had never known, making him desperately search for other lost pieces.

The ceremony had gone well, Mary Lou looked beautiful in her white wedding regalia and Lyle handsome and dapper in a black suit, with his hair slick with grease. They had looked a picture of happiness as they came through the church door, arm in arm and slowly walked through an applauding gauntlet of people. Pink and white confetti had been distributed in abundance to everybody in large boxes and had began to fly in the air and land on the happy couple, who were smiling graciously at everybody.

Suddenly Wyatt who had been standing close to them as they passed, wedged between two big farm boys became visibly alarmed. He tried to step back, but was being impeded by the crowd standing behind him. A look of dire panic had moulded his face into a mask of sheer terror, baring his large teeth into a shocking grimace. A pink rain of confetti appeared to be missing the joyful couple and landing in abundance on a by now extremely distraught Wyatt.

Everybody had noticed, and the cold feel of adrenaline had gripped Wayne's whole spectrum of feelings, because he had never seen his austere brother behaving anything like this before. But what was it? What had antagonised him, flashed through Wayne's mind. It was the confetti. The confetti, or fear of it, had thrown him into a blind, catatonic panic. Wyatt was now flaying his arms around, like broken, dislocated broomsticks, desperately trying to break free. But the rain of confetti was still in full flight and still predominantly finding Wyatt. By now he was kicking and lashing out wildly at everybody. Wayne had stepped in the centre of the aisle of shocked and completely bewildered people and had shouted,

"It's the confetti, he's frightened of the confetti!"

Wyatt somehow managed to barge an exit route through the crowd and run at incredible speed away from the scene. He looked like something akin to a demented ostrich, with his bandy, stick thin legs carrying him off. Pink confetti was still flying off his head and shoulders, as he cleared a fence like a champion hurdler and vanish through a low slung meadow, leaving a trail of pink confetti behind him.

Wayne still harboured the memory of Pat slowly walking away from the congregation and following the path of his son, with a halo of blue pipe smoke circling around his head. Wayne had tried to reassure the gathering that he would try to find out what had happened to Wyatt. But as he followed his father through the meadow a feeling of deep sympathy and pain caressed his heart and soul, if not for Wyatt, but his father. Had this been a prelude, or a dire warning, beyond his understanding of the terrible events, which were about to unfold events that he could not control.

Pat had asked Wayne not to mention the incident at the church to Wyatt, or anybody else. If Pat had gleaned anything at all from him, he was keeping it to himself. Wyatt had quietly gone back to his studying in his ramshackle study, his only visitor being Tom Boucher, who would bring books and sheets of poetry.

All in all, things settled down into the old routine for Wayne of work and sleep, with the occasional outing with Ty and Wade. Until the one night that would change Wayne's opinion of his loathsome, toothy brother forever.

It had been one of those hot, balmy summer nights, with crickets and other nocturnal creature's making their individual melodies in the clammy dark. It was two o'clock in the morning and Wayne could not sleep, despite being tired and irritable. He had sat up from the bed and walked over to the window and looked out over to the outbuildings, that were nothing more than dark outlines. The light from Wyatt's study was still burning brightly and Wayne thought that Wyatt might as well take his bed over there, because he virtually lived out there, like some weird hermit.

Suddenly Wayne had seen movement at the end of the buildings. He tried to adjust his sight to the area and sure enough somebody was moving about in the shadows. He thought that his eyes were deceiving him when Wyatt appeared from out of the dark and cautiously climbed over the wooden fencing. He was carrying a small satchel and his hat was pulled down over his head. Wayne made sure that it was Wyatt who he was watching. As the figure deftly planted his feet onto the other side of the fence Wayne could clearly see that yes it was Wyatt, the unmistakable figure of Wyatt. But what on earth could he be doing by creeping around like a thief in the night.

Wayne waited patiently for Wyatt to climb over the far fence and disappear into the dark woods and then made his way over to Wyatt's study. As he peered through the window he could see the back of Wyatt's high chair and the back of a hat. The hat had been propped up to give the impression that somebody was sitting in the chair. But Wayne could see in the reflection of the glass-fronted bureau that the hat was being propped up on a broom and the chair was empty. Several books had been splayed open on the desk to enhance the appearance of somebody studying. Wayne had thought to himself, whatever you're up to Wyatt, you sure don't trust me.

It was not until nearly four o'clock when Wyatt returned. Wayne watched him follow the same route back over the fences and quietly enter through his study door. The satchel, which had obviously been empty when he left, was now stuffed full with something.

When the light went out and Wyatt made his way back to the house Wayne had jumped quickly into bed and had feigned sleep. And as Wyatt quietly slipped his boots off and slid into his bed over the other side of the room, Wayne had been tantalizingly tempted to ask him where the hell had he been, creeping around like a thief in the night. But no, if Wyatt had secrets to keep, maybe it was because he had to. Whatever it was and whatever he had been doing, he was behaving completely out of character. Wayne was to find out the next day when a furious and half demented Ben Boucher and a posse of startled hirelings, their faces white with shock and fear turned up at the farm the next day. Boucher's face was purple with suppressed anger.

Pat had gone out to meet them, looking perplexed and puffing on his pipe robustly. The usual halo of blue smoke danced around his head as he said,

"What can I do for yah Mister Boucher? Don' usually see you round these parts."

"Maybe yah can Pat, the slave I had strung up near the house for stealing, well some son of a bitch cut him loose late last night. Was wonderin' if you or yah boys had seen anythin'... I gotta reward for any information that can bring the cuss to me."

Wayne, who was standing close behind his father, watched his reaction carefully.

"Wow, who on earth would do such a thing Mr. Boucher? Don't make sense. Ma boys were here all night. Wayne was asleep and Wyatt was studying most of the night. Did yah hear anythin', or did anythin' disturb yah last night Wayne?"

Wayne hated to see his noble father acting humble in front of a man that Wayne regarded as no better than a villain. But he was also well aware of the absolute power of Ben Boucher and the way he could bring that power to bear as he alone deemed fit. As he answered another thought had been swimming around inside of his head and it was difficult for him to be calm and collective. It could not have been Wyatt, surely? Only a complete madman would dare commit such an outrage against Ben Boucher.

"No Pa, I couldn't sleep much last night and Wyatt was studying most of the night. Went over to check the hosses 'bout four thirty, as yah know Talula is 'bout to give birth, looked in on Wyatt and he had his nose stuck in a book, that's all really."

Wayne sincerely hoped that he had come across well with his answer, then waited patiently for Boucher's next move, with cold sweat trickling down his back.

"Well Pat, I'll tell yah, as I've told everybody else so far. If and when I do catch the darn thief that stole my own thief, I'm gonna hang 'im from the highest tree."

And as Boucher galloped away, with his entourage trailing behind him Pat muttered, "I'm sure you will Ben Boucher, I'm darn sure you will."

Wayne was not watching as Boucher and his hirelings left, because his gaze was firmly fixed on the door of Wyatt's study. Surely it can't be him, surely not Wyatt?

It took two weeks for the pandemonium and scandal to subside about the stolen thief. Everybody hoped that Boucher would simmer down on his own accord and nobody wanted him to catch the thief stealer. Because woe betide that individual if he did, as everybody knew that man never made idle threats.

The only person to discover the real truth, by accident was Wayne. Wayne had dismissed the thoughts of the offender being Wyatt, simply because it did not add up. Wyatt had never shown any radical views on slavery, indeed nobody knew his views about anything. But it still remained a mystery to Wayne, as to what Wyatt was doing, creeping around during that particular night. Wyatt very nearly did get caught out though, and by sheer luck Wayne managed to foil that discovery.

Tom Boucher arrived at the farm one morning, carrying some books. He was knocking on the door of Wyatt's study, when Wayne noticed him. Wayne had casually walked over and told Tom that Wyatt was in town with Pat, but it was okay to leave the books on Wyatt's desk.

Fortunately Wayne had opened the door for Tom. Because the first thing Wayne noticed as he entered the room was the satchel under the desk. And out of it, the ends of the Boucher clan's infamous bright yellow rope were protruding.

Wayne felt as though he had been suddenly punched in the stomach. He moved quickly to plant his feet in front of the satchel, hoping desperately that Tom had not noticed it. Thankfully he had not and as Tom placed the books on the desk Wayne let rip with an explosive fart. Tom looked at Wayne in utter disgust and deferred a sharp – 'Good day sir,' and sauntered off through the door.

Wayne quickly picked the satchel up and checked the contents. Sure enough it was stuffed full of the Boucher rope, which had been cut in several places. And the other piece of damning evidence was a razor sharp knife. Wayne stuffed all of the rope back into the satchel and hid it further back, under the desk and out of sight. He then began to laugh out loud, with his nerves still on tenterhooks and cold sweat stifling his senses.

"Wyatt, you son of a gun, it was you, it was you… Well I'll be damned Wyatt…!"

Wayne had been sorely tempted to raise the subject with Wyatt about the slave, but the sheer gravity of what he had done still beggared belief in Wayne's mind. But one night as Wyatt slipped into bed, Wayne had found an alibi to deftly raise the subject.

"Was up in town today buying stores for Pa today. Yah know it's been over a month and folks are still talking 'bout that slave that some crazy dude cut free in the night."

"Really, coulda been another slave who felt pity for him," said Wyatt.

"Yeh, I thought about that, but it don't add up. The slave was strung up, real close to the Boucher house. The slave quarters are right at the other end of the plantation. Now for another slave to venture out and cross all those cotton fields in the night and not draw attention to himself, it simply could not be done."

"Why's that?" asked Wyatt cautiously.

"Coz ole Boucher's got two boys with shotguns prowling the area all night, in particular round the house and the slave quarters. Another slave nah," said Wayne.

"Then who do yah think done it then Wayne?" said Wyatt coldly.

"Must be some dude with deep felt convictions that he keeps strictly to himself. To do otherwise would be sheer suicide."

"A damn fool, if you ask me," said Wyatt with a hint of sarcasm.

"A damn brave fool, if you ask me."

"I ain't askin' you Wayne, there's a lotta boys that would give anything to work at the Boucher place. Loose talk could get you in serious trouble Wayne."

"Maybe it could, but I can't help but admire the dude that did it. The sheer daring and audacity of it, would sure like to shake that dudes hand."

"Drop the subject Wayne, the last thing Pa needs now is some darn fool blabberin' his mouth off 'bout cutting slave's loose. After all he was caught stealin.'"

"There was no proof that it was him, after all Boucher has got four other boys workin' up at the plantation who have access to his storeroom. I figure the dude that cut him loose must of taken account of that. That's why he did it. Wow."

"Nobody in their right mind would think about the rights of a slave that was caught stealin' Wayne. Most folks would think he got his just deserts."

"Not me Wyatt, nah. Nobody could stand up and trade punches with a man of Boucher's power. Musta been a dude with a strong sense of justice and duty."

"A damn fool, that's got no place meddlin' in things that ain't his business."

Wayne digested what Wyatt had said in quiet disbelief and carried on.

"He musta had some idea of the plantations layout. And he musta planned how he was gonna do it. And he damn well did it with military precision."

"Drop the subject Wayne, you're talkin' more stupid than I thought you were."

"He must of approached from the south, taking a long route. He must of crossed the stream that runs across the extreme south of the cotton fields. It musta been very difficult to cross all of those fields in the pitch dark and still keep his bearings. When he finally approached the house, how comes all those hound dogs that Boucher's got did not start barkin'?

Well, I've also thoughta that. Coz those darn hound dogs knew the intruder, he probably even stroked them. He musta also known that the two boys patrolling the estate woulda shot him without question, if they'd caught him. He also musta known that those two boys would be in serious trouble anyway if he got away with the deed. Then after cutting the slave loose he would have had to carry him over at least four acres of fields in the pitch dark, coz the boy woulda been too exhausted to walk. Then carry him across that deep stream…Now what kinda dude could do that?"

"A damn fool dude Wayne, a damn fool dude."

"A damn brave fool dude Wyatt, a damn brave fool," Wayne said, wryly.

Peach blossom and pink confetti.

War had become inevitable from the moment that General Beauregard had ordered firing on Fort Sumter. The northern protagonists in power and the southern stalwarts had been thrown into a dubious and uncompromising position. The northern invader was about to probe south and the southern defenders of a doctrine, which they had very little control of themselves were about to pitch into each other in bloody battle. The rich man's war, fought by poor boys was about to erupt across the land like a storm.

Wayne watched with guarded interest as the boys, twenty-two in all fell into a hap-hazard formation and were made ready to march off. They looked quite smart in their crisp grey uniforms, some wearing peaked forage caps and some wearing grey slouch hats.

Jolly banter and levity was manifest in the ranks and Ty and Wade were up to their usual horseplay. The only one that looked out of place was Wyatt. Wyatt's uniform did not fit him at all, the tunic was far too big and the trousers were at half-mast, barely covering his knees.

As they marched away with the crowds cheering and waving, Wayne observed how ridiculous Wyatt looked, marching at the rear completely out of step with the rest. This would be the last picture that Wayne would have of Wyatt, a picture that would tear at his heart for the rest of his life. The only reason that Wayne was not in the ranks was that the war department had taken note of his penchant for horse handling and had ordered him to take a batch over to the east. The rest of the boys had treated Wayne with sympathy when he had been detailed off. Because already General Mc Clellan had brought his massive army of the Potomac south and General Joe Johnston was shrewdly counterpunching Mc Clellan's every move. The union defeat at the first Bull run battle had forced the issue that the union must deliver a knockout blow to the confederacy and that blow had not yet landed, much to the frustration and fear by the men of the north.

Everybody in he north and south had got their predictions wrong. The army of the Potomac was being superbly boxed by Joe Johnston, until the shrewd little General had been seriously wounded at the Seven pines battle. When the semi retired General Lee had been put in Johnston's place, after being no more than a military adviser to Jefferson Davis, the fundamental question was, could General Lee measure up? At the time the hapless General Mc Clellan remarked unfortunately, that the war would be easier from now on, because Lee would be irresolute and timid. How wrong and mistaken he was.

What had happened next shocked and surprised everybody, especially General Mc Clellan. Not only had General Lee out boxed his opponents, one after the other, he had beaten them to the punch every time. Wayne could clearly remember the scene after the second Bull Run battle, when Lee was already growing into legend incarnate.

His brigade had just pushed back Fitz John Porter's rearguard action and were loitering around a captured artillery and ammunition, when there was a great roar of approval from the boys. All of the top Generals had come to congratulate them. Firstly came James Longstreet, squat, powerful and looking more like a pig farmer in his floppy hat and smock. Then the quirky looking Richard Ewell, with his big, beak-like nose and bald head, who was cordially shaking everybody's hand with great enthusiasm. And then came Thomas Stonewall Jackson, with the cold, calculating and distant eyes of a killer, who was more preoccupied in ordering the Colonel to ensure that the weaponry and ammunition was taken stock of and sent back for distribution. Then the General appeared with none other than Robert E. Lee himself. The two Generals looked quite similar in bearing and countenance, the only physical difference being that General Lee was taller, larger and a lot more greyer. Lee had removed his long white gauntlets and was shaking hands with the boys as if he was experiencing a deeply felt gratitude.

Wayne reflected how the General could not conceal his enthusiasm and pride in his boys as he glided around with Lee and all of the other Generals. That enthusiasm would slowly die as he saw more and more boys left dead on battlefields, whose names were to become synonymous with death and wholesale slaughter.

The twenty-two who all marched away in carefree abandon to join the western armies were now all dead, some buried, some never even identified in death. Wyatt and Ty were amongst the first to die. Wayne had constructed a perfect picture of their deaths from long and detailed letters from Pat. They had been killed in a peach orchard near an obscure place called Shiloh. Nobody knew the reason why General Albert Sidney Johnston had ordered the attack, after quarrelling with General Beauregard. But it was becoming very clear that after the unknown General Grant had captured Fort Henry and Fort Donelson in quick succession, swallowing up two confederate armies whole, that a big counterpunch and become a dire necessity.

General Johnston had very nearly pulled off a spectacular victory against Grant, but the unforeseen had happened and had seriously impeded the surprise attack. A sunken road that was held by federal troops, which had been deemed as not much more than a picket line, had been the scene of desperate fighting. The two lines of massed confederates could not dislodge the Federals, so they had to sweep around them. An unknown irregular General named Benjamin Prentiss had probably given Grant enough time to reorganise and rally his routed and fleeing brigades, as Prentiss and his men held the sunken road.

Wyatt and Ty had been on the right flank as they swept around the road, driving the panic stricken Federals before them. Victory had been so close, but Grant had finally managed to check the balance, despite his entire army nearly being pushed into the Tennessee River. Wyatt's brigade had finally been stopped in a peach orchard, very close to Shiloh church. Federal artillery had been mustered by the banks of the Tennessee and was laying on a heavy fire directly into the peach orchard. Heavy bombs from the Federal gun ships Tyler and Lexington that were anchored in the river were also wreaking havoc in the orchard. Peach blossom had been flying in the air like confetti as canister and shot ripped into the peach trees. When General Johnston was shot close by, the attack slowly ground to a halt. But by now the peach orchard was nothing more than a conglomeration of bloody, battered bodies, broken trees and pink peach blossom, cascading around as if it had come to celebrate a macabre wedding.

After the battle Wyatt had been found dead. He appeared to be only sleeping, face up, under a blanket of peach blossom. Only his face had been visible, shrouded by a veil of peach blossom. His waif-like body had been completely intact compared to the other boys, including Ty, who had been mutilated and decapitated beyond any recognition.

All but four of the twenty-two had died at Shiloh. Wade had been killed later on while trying to carry Snodgrass hill, at the battle of Chickamauga.

He had been one of the first to die, as Nathan Bedford Forrest and James Longstreet failed to dislodge the cool and unflappable General George Thomas and profane General Gordon Granger. The other three had been killed at Stone's river, including John Boucher, who had held the rank of Colonel at the time of his death. The only one who was still alive, apart from Wayne was Tom Boucher. He had fled to California at the beginning of the war declaring – 'That this war by comparison was tantamount to an irate husband setting fire to himself in protest, when he found out that his wife was being unfaithful.'

After four long years of war Pat and Ben Boucher had at least one thing in common, and that was that they were both broken and disenfranchised men.

CHAPTER 7

Wayne was suddenly brought back to reality by the call of the camp rooster. He had been awake for hours, pondering past and present. And as the sun began to peep through the slats of the stables he reminded himself that he had been ordered to see the General at nine o'clock sharp.

The General was already waiting for him as Wayne approached, stroking the horse, which Wayne had trained especially for him. The old man seemed delighted to see him.

"Ah private Rawlins, just wanted to congratulate you on this fine beast that you chose for me. Must say I've never handled such a clever and obedient horse. He's even better than my last one, who suffered such a terrible fate. By the way, why did you name him Jubal?"

Wayne had to hide his own amusement as he answered the General.

"After General Early Sir…I had to get the feel of him, coz he could have one furious temper if he was riled, or handled badly."

"Ah ha, Jubal Early, furious temper, now I see, just like my good friend General Early. Must say though, I've found him to be almost human in his temperament."

"That's coz he likes you Sir and you're handling him well. Otherwise he would of thrown you sky high by now Sir. A hoss ain't no dumb beast Sir, it has feelings, just like us. They can sense folk that understand and care about them."

"Well that's good to know private Rawlins, I wish you'd told me that when you brought him over. Sure don't wanna find myself providing a rodeo show for the boys."

"There's not one bad hoss in the batch, it's just gonna take some time to train 'em Sir."

"Well just keep at it private Rawlins, would like to know regular reports on their progress. Oh yes, I've got somethin' for you, come into my office."

As they walked into the office Wayne noticed the full bottle of whisky on the General's desk. The old man picked it up and handed it to Wayne and said, "That's for you, please take a seat brave boy."

Wayne sat down and wondered if the General was going to go into one of his long, elaborate speeches. He was right, but Wayne soon realised that the General needed somebody to talk to. Wayne really did not want to talk, instead he just listened, as the General produced a large tumbler and poured himself a shot of whisky from a hip flask.

"Would you like some?" asked the General casually.

"No thanks Sir, it's a bit too early for me."

"What do you think brave boy? How long do you think we're gonna last now? Lee is trapped in front of Petersburg, with his thin lines stretched to the limit. And the Federals are piling on every resource to break through. The railway lines feeding Petersburg have been destroyed. Federal cavalry is probing well behind our lines, causing havoc. Schofield has destroyed half of Hood's army at Franklin. Thomas has completely destroyed the rest of it at Nashville. Sherman is rampaging up through, and ransacking the whole of Georgia and is about to do the same in South Carolina. Joe Johnston is trying to muster the remnants of several smashed armies just to try and stop Sherman. How long do you think we can hold on?"

Wayne did not have to contemplate his thoughts and his answer was very clear.

"Well Sir, the only hope in hell we got is if General Lee can break away from Petersburg, join up with General Johnston, beat General Sherman, then turn on General Grant. But then, I doubt if even General Lee could turn things round now."

"Quite right, quite right, I never thought that it would last this long though. Every time you think it's only a matter of time for us, Lee pulls off some brilliant counterstroke and completely throws Federal strategy. But not this time, not this time."

Wayne quietly observed the General's manner and countenance and noticed the marked contrast in that manner after four years of hard war.

The old man went on,

"I've seen my best officers killed, I've killed fine officers that were friends at West point. And I was damn well told many years before that it would happen, but I never thought in my worst nightmares that it would be anything like this."

He then went into deep thought and spoke as if he was reflecting on a profound secret.

"It would have been in the summer of eighteen fifty. I was up in Ohio visiting my wife's uncle, the good Reverend Leopold Blunt. We were sitting at the front of his house, in his well-kept gardens. It was a warm summer evening, with young children running barefoot through the meadows, next to his beloved gardens. Some of the children were swinging on the branches of his trees that were hanging over the fence. He had noticed this himself, but he had said nothing, which was unusual because he was famously cantankerous towards all children. Even when one of the branches broke off from one of his trees, he didn't seem angry, he just stared over to the children blankly. I was thinking that his heart condition was nullifying his reactions, because his normal reaction, knowing his character, would have been one of uncontrollable anger. Trying to gauge the feel of his mood I remarked that it reminded me of my home down in old Virginia, with young children prancing about barefoot through meadows and gardens, without a care in the world. He just looked at me, with his eyes boring into me and said, 'Let them play, let them play, because they will be the innocent victims of our sins, in perhaps ten years time. I asked him what on earth he was talking about, because he was well aware of my opinions on theology and religion. He repeated his words, let them play, let them play. Whether it be here, in Virginia or Washington, wherever. Because most of the boys will be buried in far off lands and most of the girls, brides waiting for ghost husbands, in just a few years time. I asked him what had inspired such pessimistic thoughts. His reply was, the same gut feeling that made him join the church, far off insights and being conscious of the devil that lurks in the hearts of guilty men.

A black cloud is looming over this country and when it sweeps down and descends upon us, it will bring death and disaster beyond belief. I told him to cheer up, as things were by no means certain, thankfully we are living in a democracy. His reply was cold and calculated. Remember my words Ambrose, this country is about to be visited by a war so horrible, so vile, that the men who unleash it will quickly lose control of it, as it takes on a monstrous life of its own. I took stock of his words, but did not ponder them unduly. He told me that he sincerely did not want to be alive to bear witness to it, and he got his wish. Because ten years later, on the day war was declared, I went up to Ohio, to his church to say goodbye. I found the old swine dead, dead in his pulpit, standing up. On his face was not the grimace of a death mask, but a grin, yes a grin, as if to say, 'I told you so Ambrose, I told you so.' His words have haunted me during every battle, every gruelling march and every time I bear witness to young men strewn over blood soaked fields. I was standing next to General Lee when the morning mist cleared at Fredericksburg when he said, 'It is well that war is so terrible, lest we grow too fond of it,' as the Federals were massacred by General Jackson in the fields before the stone wall. And in the same breath he said to Jubal Early, 'Now it's your turn, my bad old man.' And that bad old man just laughed and drove his troops down from the heights, driving the Federals before him. I've been with General Longstreet as he has herded his troops like a pig farmer into the Federal lines, with the Federal Generals bobbing about like buoys on a blue sea; only to be blown to pieces by cannon fire. And through all of this the words of the good Reverend Leopold Blunt have come back to haunt me like a cantankerous ghost, 'I told you so Ambrose.'"

CHAPTER 8

Luke was not measuring up and Wayne had been losing his temper with him. Luke was intimidated by Wayne's constant chastising had his stutter was becoming worse. Wayne could indeed be intimidating to anybody, in particular to a shy boy of sixteen.

After years of living off salt pork, hard tack and dirty water; eating the camp food had filled out Wayne's frame with lean, hard muscle. His corn blond hair and fresh complexion was aglow from drinking copious amounts of fresh water from the well and mountain stream. It was not that he disliked Luke, he was just becoming frustrated by Luke not digesting and learning from his instructions.

Unknown to both of them, somebody had quietly been listening and watching Wayne's antics from a thick glade of trees that rose up at the far end of the stables. That person had become quite amused by the way that Wayne would shout.

"Don't be afraid of him Luke, he can see and sense you're afraid of him. Yah gotta show him who's boss. You'll never tame hosses if they know you're scared of 'em!"

The part that would amuse the unseen observer in particular was when Wayne would speak soothingly and almost apologetically to the poor boy, after he had finally carried out Wayne's instructions properly. This blond haired, savage looking man had been slowly lapping at the shores of somebody's subconscious, like slow moving waves probing a lonely beach. Belinda had noticed Wayne, even before he had even seen her.

Belinda could have easily gone down and told the ferocious looking white man, that it was actually him frightening the boy more than the horses were. But she had checked herself by thinking that a man might not take too kindly to a woman telling him what the problem was, in particular a black woman. However Wayne's scolding and verbal abuse became less frequent, as Luke finally began to overcome his fear of Wayne and the horses.

Belinda had begun to observe with guarded interest a more tender side to Wayne's exterior, tough countenance, especially as Luke's confidence grew in skips and bounds. She would notice Wayne cheering and laughing with abandon, as Luke was being bucked and jostled by a semi wild horse, until the horse was finally brought to bear. Something was stirring and waking up deep inside of her, but she did not know what it was. She had originally found solace up in the glade every afternoon, after she had finished working with the other women. She had very little time for pointless chatter and trivial gossip that the other dispossessed slave women indulged in, so she would take her father's bible, or another book and wile away her spare time reading. The glade was a perfect spot for somebody seeking solitude, with the sound of the flowing river far below on one side and the stables and pens on the other. It had not even occurred to her that an obscure ulterior motive had crept in through the back doors of her heart. But it had begun to grow more apparent to her when she slowly realised that she was spending more time watching the blond, athletic and very mobile man, than studying her bible. What had fascinated her about him in particular was the marked contrast of barbarian and a peculiar trait of kindness. This trait would rise to the surface when he was handling the horses, or when he appeared to feel guilty, after giving the boy a very hard day's lesson in horse handling. This trait in a man she had only ever seen in her father and very rarely in her former master's son, Joshua.

She could show Luke a thing or two about horses herself, which she had learnt as a child from her father and Joshua. She could empathise with Luke, because she had feared horses, or rather the sheer size of them herself. But long excursions through the savannahs below South Carolina with her father and Joshua, where she would spend hours in the saddle, had completely quelled that fear. Yet even in her father and Joshua she had not seen this deep love and understanding of horses that this man had.

Unfortunately Belinda's first close encounter with Wayne would be under ugly and violent circumstances.

And although Wayne had still not noticed her when those circumstances had erupted, her own emotions would jump from ones which were like by comparison, waves that were gently lapping at the distant shores of her subconscious, to waves crashing on the immediate beach of her conscious.

Wayne and Luke had taken some horses down to the river for watering. Further up the river where the water passed through some stony shallows, they could hear some of the former slave women chattering and laughing as they tended to their washing. Neither Wayne nor Luke had been paying much attention as the horses drank, when suddenly the women started screaming with fear. They tethered the horses to some trees and went to see what all of the commotion was about. As they approached they saw a scrawny old timer, with a big black patch over his left eye, trying in vain to wrestle a long whip from a big, fat brawny man called Clayton. Clayton shoved the old timer away, but he came back and grabbed hold of Clayton's arm again. This time Clayton punched him and the old man fell heavily to the ground. Clayton had obviously been terrorising the women with the whip and was about to proceed, when the whip was pulled from his hand and thrown far out into the river. Although Clayton was facing the other way, the sheer force of the wrench warned him that it was not the old timer apprehending him this time. He turned to face Wayne and met cold blue eyes boring into his own. The old timer although still concussed, leapt between Wayne and Clayton and was joined by a startled Luke. The old man spoke with the bile of hatred.

"You never change Clayton, you never change…Treating the Yankee prisoners badly ain't good enough for yah, you can't even leave these poor women alone yah bastard."

Clayton ignored the old man and kept his whole attention on Wayne. Wayne did not speak, his eyes told Clayton everything he needed to know.

"Well, well horse boy, don't yah like to see some slave women being whipped? Got no stomach for it. Better stick to yah hosses then, coz yah may get whipped yah self."

Wayne remained cold and impassive, but the killer in him had been quickly awoken.

"I've seen too much whippin' in ma life, but it takes a real bad son of a bitch to whip helpless women, a real mother fuckin' son of a bitch."

"Yah think I'm afraid of yah horse boy. Maybe I should whip yah too, horse boy."

Wayne was winning the war on nerves, his tone remained cold and impassive and Clayton had already sampled Wayne's rapier speed and strength.

"Be my guest hog shit, just try."

Clayton did not try to push the old timer away this time as he stood between him and Wayne, and a very anxious Luke quickly moved to put himself in their path as well.

As Clayton walked away, Luke breathed a deep sigh of relief. The old timer adjusted his eye patch and spoke to the still distraught women.

"Okay ladies, it's all over now, yah can carry on with yah chores, it's all okay."

He then turned to Wayne and Luke, surveying them with his hawk-like good eye and put his gnarled and work-worn hand out.

"I'd sure like to thank you fellas, the name's Jed Wallace. I came in with Clayton and two others from Braxton Bragg's old army. Clayton is bein' moved out to join the Petersburg lines soon. I know him well and he ain't nothing but trouble."

Wayne introduced himself and Luke, then calmly said,

"Well that's okay Jed, you can rely on me and my buddy Luke if you need any help."

Luke's face lit up and his heart filled with pride as the word, 'buddy' entered his ears like a symphony. At last Wayne was beginning to treat him like a man and a buddy. And in the middle of the crew of washerwomen, somebody else's heart had been touched.

One of the women had to nudge Belinda, because her eyes were involuntarily fixed on the every move, every gesture and every word of the wild, yet majestic blond man.

"What's the matter gal, yah look as if you're in love."

She then nudged Belinda again and winked at her, slyly.

"Mind you, can't say as I blame yah gal, he sure is a fine lookin' dude."

"He ain't no dude Polly, he is, he is, he is."

"He's just a man. All men are the same gal, dude or no dude. Their carnal deeesires drive them all to distraction and I mean deeestraction. All gals are the same to them."

Polly nudged Belinda and winked at her again.

"Now get back to work gal, before you go into a swoon."

A week later Wayne picked up two empty buckets and trundled off to fill them up from the well that was on the parameters of dilapidated buildings. He was vaguely aware of the young black woman as he approached who was leaning over the well, hauling out a heavy bucket full of water. He immediately noticed her strong shapely legs, which extended from a short white robe. And then he noticed her shapely but strong arms, which were taut with the weight of the bucket. She had not seen him coming and had gracefully kicked away a stone with the sole of her barefoot, which rolled towards him. Her big breasts were moving about, beneath the robe, clutching and releasing her bosom as she toiled. Only when Wayne came up to the well did she notice him. And when she did she appeared to be slightly alarmed to see him.

Never before in his life had Wayne seen such a really beautiful woman. He had seen many attractive women and many that he would term as cute and pretty women. Ones that could be charming and sedate in their frocks and frills, but this was the first time he had seen a really graceful and beautiful woman. Belinda was the first to speak.

"I'm sorry, I didn't see you coming."

"You got no reason to be sorry, I didn't mean to creep up on yah like that."

"I kicked the stone without looking, thought nobody was about at this time."

Wayne was having difficulty absorbing a whole swarm of unusual feelings. She looked like an Egyptian queen that had jumped out of one of Wyatt's books and come to life. Her high cheekbones and large brown eyes that slanted up slightly highlighted a face, which was breathtakingly beautiful. Her hair was bunched up on top of her head and fastened with a violet band, revealing the full beauty of her face.

Her skin was slightly darker than the other former slave women and shone like silk.

"Can I help yah? That's some heavy bucket you're liftin'," said Wayne, trying to appear as casual as he could be.

"Well that sure is kind of yah, if yah really don't mind."

For some strange reason, Wayne began to feel the awkward pangs of embarrassment and he could feel warm blood creeping up to his ears. He certainly did not want her to think that there was an ulterior motive in his offer and his face was dealt another dose of warm blood as he realised there was. He had never experienced these overpowering feelings of delectation to a woman before and he was having great difficulty negotiating them. As he concentrated his efforts on pulling the full pale of water from the well, he could feel her eyes watching his every move, probing and scrutinising each move with open interest. As he handed her the pale of water, she thanked him and walked away.

Belinda had to hide her smile as she walked, because she could feel his eyes watching her every move. He had noticed her, he had noticed her and for the first time in her life she had realised that she was a beautiful woman.

CHAPTER 9

Wayne sat at the back of the gathering, supping thoughtfully on the cloudy beer. He could see that the boys sitting close to the campfire were listening with interest at Clayton's stories. Orange flames cast dancing shadows across their puzzled faces as Clayton's stories began to border on being gross exaggerations, as he seemed to put himself in pivotal roles in each battle. Wayne vaguely listened but his mind was somewhere else. He could not get her out of his head, although he had been trying to.

"When General Cleburne fell against me with blood pouring from his chest and said, How are we doin' Jake? I just said, we've lost five other Generals Pat and five thousand boys. The Yankees have got too many heavy guns in the second line, don't think we can break through like we did the first line. Soon afterwards General Hood pulled us out, but we put up one hellova fight."

Jed Wallace was visibly cringing with embarrassment, with his face screwed up and his shoulders bunched up close to his ears. His whole manner told the gathering everything – How on earth do you expect these boys to believe that tall story Clayton? You weren't even in the Franklin battle. You were the first to volunteer for ambulance duty. – But before the story had finished Wayne was already making his way back to the stables. He would try to sleep again, but her face, those eyes, that dark silk-like skin, her magnificent and graceful body and those breasts moving about under that scanty, short white robe would be in his thoughts again and he knew it.

He had seriously been contemplating planning some kind of meeting with her. But how could he instigate such a meeting, without it looking as though he had a surreptitious motive. He did indeed have a very clear and defined ulterior motive, he wanted her and he wanted her badly. His thoughts had been nothing like hers, and they were not like waves lapping at a distant shore and moving in on his feelings like a probing tidal flow. Her presence and her whole countenance at the well were indelibly stamped on his mind and was driving him to distraction.

He had gone to the well on several occasions with empty buckets even when the horse troughs were completely full of water. But his bogus reason for doing this had not brought him into contact with her again. And in frustration one day he had kicked a bucket in the air, narrowly missing a somewhat bewildered Luke. Powerful desires were now turning into cruel obsessions.

Belinda had no reason to go to the well again and it would look extremely suspicious to the other women, if she grabbed an empty bucket and made a bee line for the well when this noticeably handsome man went to collect water. The marked contrast in her two close experiences with him had been playing on her mind. And those red ears of a man who was obviously self conscious in the presence of a woman had amused her, when she remembered that cold, calculating same man concerning the incident down by the river. Her next encounter with him would be an even a bigger shock to her system.

Luke had been tending the horses that day and she had noticed that Wayne had been giving the boy more responsibility for the horses as Luke's confidence grew. She had gone to the glade later than usual that particular afternoon, because of the workload that had been growing steadily as the camp had become more transient in recent times. She had noticed that Wayne was not present around the stables that afternoon and vaguely wondered where he was. After reading for a while she had decided to take a walk along the river. As she walked down through the bushes and trees she saw him. He was stark naked, vigorously washing himself in the shallows. She tried to tear herself away, but she couldn't. He was facing the other way and his white muscular buttocks were bobbing up and down alternately as he scrubbed himself.

Again she tried to tear herself away, but she could not take her eyes off him and his movements. Her heart began to flutter wildly and she began to feel like a child that was doing something forbidden and very naughty. She quickly made sure that she was well covered by greenery, just in case he turned around and saw her. He then plunged his whole body into the water and stood up again, throwing his wet hair back.

His white skin was glistening in the late afternoon sunlight, as the sparkling water trickled down his taut, muscular body. Once again she tried to tear herself away, but she couldn't, because he was magnificent, absolutely magnificent. She did not know what these foreign, peculiar feelings were, but they were far too strong for her. He plunged into the water again and stood up, but this time the cascading water dazzled her vision and she briefly lost sight of him as he splashed about. Pangs of deep desire began to penetrate down through her solar plexus and she could feel and hear her heart beating rapidly. She tried to retreat back through the greenery, but her legs had become weak and she briefly lost her balance. She swallowed and realised that her mouth had become parched and dry. Her hands felt clammy and she could feel sweat tickling her sides as it trickled down from her armpits. She tried to pull herself together and make a concerted effort to escape. What if he saw her? What would he think? What on earth had come over her? Just as she thought she had mustered the strength to pull away he turned around. She instantly became riveted to the spot and her arms and legs felt like lead weights. He rubbed his hair and shook his head about, his shapely pectoral and shoulder muscles stretching and contracting in unison. Her eyes dropped down to his taut, flat stomach muscles, then down to his manhood. Belinda had never seen a naked man before and it was ironic that her first introduction to one was to be of a well-endowed man. And the owner of that manhood was a man she wanted badly.

All hope of pulling away now had left her as she watched and savoured every inch of his body. He looked as if he had been carved out of white marble, with every line cut with great care by a master sculptor. Suddenly he began to walk towards the shore taking long, lunging steps, with his manhood swinging around like a long, stout pendulum. It dawned on her abruptly that she must withdraw now, before he saw her. Then just as abruptly, as these thoughts crossed her tormented emotions, he turned at a right angle and walked in a straight line, directly towards her hideout. Only then did she notice his clothes piled up, directly beneath her position.

Fear of being caught finally transcended every other feeling, which had caught her off guard and she rapidly backed off through the shrubbery and trees. Only then did she realise that she was trembling and shaking from head to toe.

Cold sweat was creating a moist film over her entire body, with warm sweat dripping from her armpits. Her legs were still like jelly and as her heart beat slowly began to settle back to its normal rate, she became slowly aware that her loins were soaking wet.

As Wayne grabbed his towel, he thought he heard movement up in the bushes above him. He looked up and saw some branches from an overhanging tree dancing around, indicating that they had been disturbed by somebody or something. He did not give this a second thought as he put his clothes on. Who would be spying on a man taking a bath anyway? The encounter that he had been planning and presiding over had happened and he did not even know it. He would go to his bed again this night and he knew that she would be on his mind again, her and everything about her.

It was Belinda's turn to brood and lose sleep this time. As she lay in bed that night, she ran through and savoured the scene by the river, over and over again. Polly had been right; she did not only look like she was in love, she was in love, and she had no control or desire to shake off these alien and powerful feelings.

CHAPTER 10

It was about midday on the following day when Jed Wallace sauntered over to Wayne and Luke as they were grooming some horses. Jed nodded anxiously and said,

"Good day to yah, Wayne, Luke."

"Mornin' Jed, what can we do for yah?" said Wayne.

"Well, I'll come right to the point Wayne."

"Go on Jed, what's eatin' yah?"

"I'm worried 'bout Clayton, real worried about Clayton."

"Awe don't worry 'bout Clayton Jed, I've seen the likes of him before."

"Oh, I doubt if you've met anybody like Clayton Wayne, he's real trouble."

"What harm can he do Jed? Besides, he's off up to Petersburg soon."

"Oh, he's off up to Petersburg all right, but he won't be doing any fightin'...Ambulance duty maybe, cookhouse duty maybe, but definitely no fighting, I know him so well."

"Well at least we'll be rid of him Jed, can't ask more than that."

Jed adjusted his eye patch and looked carefully at Wayne through his good eye. He then pointed at his bad eye with a bony finger and said,

"See that, my eye is bad and it's getting worse. See the other two boys that come in with Clayton and me, they have both been wounded, one in the chest, one in the leg. Now what do yah notice 'bout Clayton? There ain't a mark on him, no sir."

"I didn't notice that Jed, not 'til you just mentioned it," said Wayne.

"Most folks don't, they're too busy listenin' to tall stories 'bout battles that he was never in. Wanna know the real reason why he's here?"

"Why's that Jed?" asked Luke and Wayne together.

"Coz it's his price of freedom for exposin' six deserters, who were hiding from the militia in a barn after the Nashville battle. He had deserted himself and was with them.

He got caught raiding a farmhouse by himself. The others may of escaped, but Clayton traded them in for his own freedom. That's why he was drafted away from all of the boys that knew what he did. He's always been a straggler and grafter, but he had never quite deserted. The six boys were all shot, everybody knew why Clayton wasn't."

"Wow, so all those stories he comes out with are lies," said Luke.

By now Wayne had sensed that Jed had more on his mind than he was letting on and wanted to know what all of this was leading up to. Jed looked worried as he carried on,

It's only a question of time now. We're losing, we're losing this war and neither Lee, Johnston or anybody else can turn it round now. Clayton has been abusing the Yankee prisoners badly, real badly. We will all be at the mercy of the Yankee soldiers when they arrive, but Clayton will be long gone and we'll all have to pay, I know it."

"Well, what can I do Jed? Can't the other boys stop him, or inform on him?"

"Clayton volunteers for duty. The other few that guard the prisoners know what he's doin', but seem powerless to stop him. The boys look up to you Wayne they don't know me. Hell, I never wanted to fight in the first place, god dammit."

"Well, thanks for the warnin' Jed, I'll think it over. Maybe the Colonel should know about Clayton, or even the General. Have you thought 'bout that?"

"If the Colonel or anybody in command is alerted, he will turn it all around in his favour and use it against the informers. I know him so damn well."

As Jed sauntered away again Luke asked Wayne, "Do yah think it's true Wayne?"

"What? About Clayton abusing the prisoners."

"No, 'bout us losin' the war."

"We're losin' alright Luke, just hope it ends soon, that's all."

Wayne did not have to wait long for his next confrontation with Clayton, and his well-tested instincts with men in the same ilk as Clayton would tell him that it would have to result in a showdown. As Wayne and Luke walked back from the canteen to go back to work Clayton's voice hailed them from a porch, where he was loitering with a few boys.

"Well, well it's the horse boy with his baby horse boy in tow, 'bout all he's good for, tendin' to dumb hosses and feedin' 'em. Combat and battle is not for the likes of him."

Clayton stepped heavily from the porch steps and sauntered out towards the centre of the dusty square, with his thumbs hooked in his belt, scratching his over-hanging belly.

The arrogant sneer warned Wayne that Clayton had found the courage to confront him. The incident by the river must have been playing on his mind.

"What's up horse boy? Lost for words. Don't care for the words of a real veteran."

"Can't say as I do care 'bout the words of a veteran ambulance volunteer and accomplished straggler. Pity they don't give medals for those duties Clayton, coz your coat would be weighed down by 'bout five hundred."

Just then Jed Wallace appeared out of the shadows of the porch and snarled at Clayton, "Drop it now Clayton, you forget I know all 'bout yah, and I'm sure all these boys would wanna know the truth. Now git back to yah…Aaahh."

Jed did not get the chance to finish, as Clayton sent him sprawling with a hard punch. He collapsed like a sack of bones down into the dust. By now Wayne was ready for Clayton, as his adrenaline geared him up for a fight. The killer in him had awoken.

"That's about your mark Clayton, hittin' ole men. Or maybe whippin' poor women."

"Or even horse boys, or maybe you'd be better tendin' chickens, or are yah one?" Clayton then began to chuckle and started making the noise of a clucking chicken. But he stopped abruptly as Wayne's next remark visibly stung him.

"Or even hogs, or hog shit like you Clayton."

"Why you son of a bitch, I'll tear your damn head off, horse boy."

"Be my guest Clayton, it would be the first time you'd faced a man in battle. I heard your ass in so full of bullets from runnin' away at Stone's river, Chattanooga, Franklin and Nashville, yah can't even sit down."

Wayne was deliberately goading Clayton in a manner as to force him to fight, while coldly gauging Clayton's exploding point. And it worked exactly as Wayne wanted. Some of the boys began to gather round and the ones who knew Wayne well, knew Clayton was in serious trouble, despite having the advantage of being a far bigger man.

Clayton suddenly lunged at Wayne, swinging a looping punch. Wayne easily sidestepped it and brought his right fist up so hard into Clayton's stomach, that Clayton staggered to one side. They then began to circle each other like prize fighters. Clayton was deceptively agile for a big, heavy man and his next punch came across so hard and fast it sent Wayne reeling. Wayne desperately tried to gather his senses as another punch caught him hard in the eye and sent him staggering backwards. Clayton was grinning as he gained confidence and Wayne could feel his right eye closing over. Wayne realised that he must use Clayton's size against him and as Clayton came forward again Wayne dodged to his left, bobbed down and threw a straight right hand punch with all of his weight behind it. It landed flush on Clayton's left jaw, breaking it with a muffled snap. Clayton gasped with pain, dropping his hands briefly. This was all that Wayne needed and he flew at Clayton, laying hard, scathing punches to his head and face. Clayton tried to cover his face and kick Wayne in the groin, but Wayne grabbed his leg and threw him in the air. As Clayton landed heavily on his back, he felt Wayne's hard boot, smash into his head, leaving him concussed. As he slipped into oblivion Wayne's words echoed around his head. It's all over Clayton, it's all over.

CHAPTER 11

"See you're a student of the bible," said Wayne, trying to sound congenial.

Belinda, who was sitting under a tree with her legs bunched up under her chin, let the bible slip from her hands, as her attention was sharply disturbed. She looked up and saw an awkward looking Wayne standing close by, with a towel draped around his neck. It took her a while to adjust herself to the surprising situation.

"Yes Sir and a lot of other books, but the bible is the one book that my father would always say, 'whatever question you have, whatever problem you can't solve, the answer is in here somewhere. It may be difficult to find, or come in a veiled way, but somewhere in these pages, there is an answer, for everybody.'"

"Sorry, can see I disturbed yah agin, like I did at the well. Just didn't expect to see anybody up here. And please don't call me sir, the name is Wayne, Wayne Rawlins."

"I know your name, Polly told me, she asked the gentleman with the patch over his eye, after the incident down by the river."

Wayne looked genuinely surprised and said,

"Really, I didn't see yah at the time."

"Well you wouldn't have, you were too preoccupied protectin' us from that bad man. I was in the middle and we all sure appreciate what yah did for us."

Wayne became visibly embarrassed by her words and he could feel his ears beginning to burn with a sudden rush of warm blood again, just like with the first encounter by the well. But he had also noticed that she had used the words preoccupied and appreciate, which told him that she was well read and quite articulate.

"Awe, it was nothin', ole Jed and Luke had an equal part in the dust-up."

On hearing this she openly smiled at him and Wayne felt that he had taken a giant skip and jump in the direction of befriending her. He was trying not to pay open attention to her cleavage and shapely legs when she stood up and looked closely at his face.

"What happened to yah eye?"

"Oh, just another incident with the same fella, that's all."

She gently touched the underneath of his eye and that touch sent a shock through his whole body. This was the first time in his life that he had sensed the deeply felt tenderness of a woman and he did not know how to handle it.

"It's swollen, but can't see any serious damage, can yah see okay outa it?"

"Yeh, I can see okay, it's gone down to what it was."

Wayne then looked around, silently observing the picturesque plot.

"Sure is peaceful up here, can see why yah come here. It's the first time I've taken the time to walk up here and I only work down there in the stables."

"I know you do, with that poor boy I always see yah with."

Wayne wondered how long she had been coming to this place, because if it had been for some weeks, then she certainly would of heard him lambasting and terrorising Luke. Belinda smiled as if she knew precisely what he was thinking.

"I'm sorry, I meant to ask yah name down at the well, but it slipped mah mind when yah left, that's been naggin' me ever since, I haven't seen yah about agin."

"My name is Belinda, Wayne, Belinda. I thought you were never gonna ask me."

Wayne felt in a state fluctuating between embarrassment and sheer delight.

"Well Belinda, I was just goin' down to mah favourite place down by the river. Would yah care to join me for a walk."

"Well, why, sure I would Wayne, sure I would." As they walked down the hill, through the trees, Wayne wondered why she was smiling wryly to herself. She had already seen him in his favourite place, in all of his glory and stark naked.

Belinda sensed that Wayne was having difficulty striking up further conversation and wondered if he had seen her spying on him while he was bathing. But she dismissed these thoughts, because his next sentence revealed the reason why.

"I notice you use words that most folks I know don't use, or don't know how to use when speaking to other folks."

For some reason she looked slightly relieved and answered him as casually and articulately as any Sunday school teacher or well-educated person that he knew.

"That's because I had the most excellent and patient teacher that anybody could ask for, my father. He made me study, and I also went to school every day until I was sixteen. Does that surprise you?"

Wayne was suffering another pang of embarrassment, and a pleasant smell of musk from his day's labour wafted in Belinda's direction, which she found rather pleasing.

"Wow, my mother wanted me to study like mah brother Wyatt, but I felt more at home working on the farm. I was more like mah pa, learnin' was not really mah vocation. I used to browse through some of Wyatt's books, but study, me, nah."

She looked him straight in the face, the closeness of her and being alone with her was still having a kind of delayed feeling of unbelievable good luck. She smiled and said,

"Well, you've obviously had some education, otherwise you wouldn't be using the words, vocation or browse, for sure. Are you being honest with me?"

She noticed that his ears were turning slightly red and felt that maybe she had been slightly harsh or misunderstood by her last words.

"Nah, what I really meant was, I was never educated to the standard of Wyatt. I went to school like other folks, but compared to Wyatt, well, his nose was always in a book. Why, he could tell you all 'bout Plato, Socrates, Leonardo Da Vinci and all of those other Greek and Italian dudes. Compared to him, me, educated, nah."

"Well, you must have had some interest, or you would never know the names of all those Greek and Italian dudes," she said, barely hiding her amusement.

"As I said, I would sometimes browse through what he was readin' when I found an open book on his table, just to try to see why he couldn't keep his nose outa books."

"That's why you were lookin', coz as my father used to say, there's part of us deep down inside that needs to learn and needs to find out. If all of us could get a good education, to read and write, then our whole view of the world about us would be far richer and we could see our true selves, like looking at your own reflection in a deep pool of clear water. Where's your brother Wyatt now, by the way?"

"He's dead. He got killed at a place called Shiloh, near the Tennessee River."

"I'm so sorry, I shouldn't of asked, please excuse me."

Wayne was scanning the river, with distant and melancholic eyes through the trees.

"That's okay, I'm sorry too. Just wish we'd got to know each other before he went and got himself killed. It's so damn funny when you think you know somebody so well and in truth you know nothing 'bout them. He was one real brave dude, real brave.

The river had begun to sparkle in the afternoon sun, as the sun peeped tantalizingly through the maples and tall oaks on the opposite bank. Here the banks sloped up sharply, taking the shape of a sheer bluff. Brush, bushes and overgrown greenery made the approach quite difficult.

But as they pushed their way through and came walking down onto ground less densely barred by shrubbery, she could see the rocky cove where she had seen him splashing about in the water. And on the far side of that cove she could see her former vantage point of observation. And yes, it was well covered by dense greenery and low slung pines. As she looked back into his face, he wondered why she smiling so serenely. If only he knew.

As Wayne walked across the square to go back to the stables, the evidence of his conversation with Belinda was being clearly displayed. A cluster of semi invalid and half starved men were passing through the main walkway, following a rickety old wagon, whose bony and badly shod horses were in no better condition than the men. It was a familiar scene for Wayne. Men who were young, robust men four years ago, reduced to tired and broken old men, within a short space of time. They would be replaced by real old men and teenage boys, marching the other way, probably to fill the ranks of these war warn veterans. Only to be killed or wounded in a half flooded trench, or dusty field. The look on the veteran's faces told the story clearly, the blank expressionless mask of defeat. These men would never brag or boast theatrical stories of fantastic battles like Clayton, because they had been in real battles, in a real war. Who had lived and suffered things far beyond their worst nightmares. Every one of them had lost a Wade, a Ty, or even a Wyatt. And every one of them had seen good and noble men die for reasons and plots that were not of their doing. So many would be brides, were now widows, in the north and south. And the dramatic picture the Reverend Leopold Blunt had painted for the General all of those years ago, could not have been expressed in a more eloquent and dramatic way.

He tried to cast these thoughts aside and focus his mind back to the previous two hours. Belinda was not only very beautiful, she was also very intelligent and sensitive. It had still not fully registered in his mind, that the endless plots and ploys that he had been planning and scheming as he lay on his bunk at night had happened purely by chance. And it could not of happened in a better and more convenient way.

What had made him take a different and more longer route to his usual bathing spot down by the river, was still a mystery to himself. He certainly could not believe his luck when he saw her sitting underneath tree, reading her bible. And her lithe, lovely legs, her voluptuous body, her breasts and her beautiful face. He had just had to stand there and take in her full, magnificent countenance before he disturbed her. And when he had disturbed her, why had he behaved with such reserve, after all she was just a woman, but what a woman. And when she touched the swelling under his eye, why had he felt as though he was melting. Tomorrow he must approach her differently, because she had been openly more at ease than he was. When they had walked, she had moved very close to him, without any fear or trepidation of being alone with a man. What was it that had amused her about him? Because that smile had implied that she knew something about him. But what could she know about him, other than what he had told her? He had earnestly wanted to tell that she looked like an Egyptian Queen, straight out of one of Wyatt's encyclopaedia's, but what kind of damn fool would say something like that to a woman who he was half mad to impress. And those stirrings in his trousers! What the hell was he playing at, behaving like a dirty dog, thank God she hadn't noticed. Yes, tomorrow he would try to be convivial, without acting like a clown. Tomorrow he must not make any mistakes he would be ready.

Belinda had been far more relaxed as she reflected on the pleasant afternoon, down by the river. Her woman's intuition had told her clearly that he wanted her and he wanted her badly. She was happy and content to savour her female power, which had been woken up quite unexpectedly. Tomorrow afternoon she would exercise it some more, with a little more daring. What had brought him up to her hideaway she didn't know and didn't care. As she entered the kitchen where Polly was busily toiling over steaming pots on a cooker, she was smiling to herself. When Polly noticed her and her manner, she eyed her suspiciously and said sarcastically,

"Whatyah smilin' at gal? No don't answer. I know that kinda smile, when I see it."

Wayne watched the sad procession disappear in a cloud of dust, their ghostly shadows moving about as if they were suspended in the sweeping dust. He slowly turned away and walked back towards the stables, remembering that he had told Luke that he would be back about six o'clock and it was now seven thirty. As he turned around the wooden buildings and looked out into the pens, he saw Luke gingerly climbing onto the back of a dangerously volatile young stallion that had been recently been brought in. He stopped and watched with interest and some trepidation as Luke soothed the horse by stroking it and speaking to it in low and slow syllables that he had learnt from Wayne. As Luke slowly lowered himself down onto the broad, powerful horse's back, it suddenly reared up without any warning and Luke had to hang onto the reins tightly and brace his legs to stop himself from being thrown clear into the air.

Wayne muttered to himself, as his adrenaline began to surge through his veins.

"Go on Luke, this is your chance to prove yah can do it. If yah can break this one, yah can break any hoss, if yah can just do this one. Go on Luke, show me yah can do it."

Even by Wayne's judgement this horse was very raw and volatile and it had that one ingredient in its character, which Wayne had learnt from years of keeping horses. And that was, it had the instinct of knowing how to throw any would be rider. But Luke was holding on and negotiating every leap and jarring lunge with skill, which Wayne had not seen in him before. He was being tossed clean out of the saddle and slung in different directions, with whiplash speed. But still he held on with grim determination. Now Wayne was watching Luke in awe and admiration, because he knew that even he, with all of his experience, would have great difficulty breaking this particular horse.

Amazingly the horse was showing no sign of losing momentum and there was no indication whatsoever that its stamina was being tested. Now Wayne slowly climbed up onto the fencing, without taking his eyes off Luke and the horse.

Luke's face had become twisted into a mask of sheer concentration, but the fury and strength of the rampaging beast was noticeably draining his strength. Wayne thought that it was only a question of time before Luke would be thrown and hoped he would not be trampled, or land badly from a whiplash sling. But incredibly, each time it looked as though Luke was about to take a tumble, he would somehow pull himself back into the saddle and tug desperately at the reins. Wayne could not contain himself any longer and began to shout and Luke grinned as he realised Wayne was watching him.

"Go on Luke, yah can do it, he's gotta tire soon, don't let him throw yah!"

But the horse was not tiring, it was growing in strength and determination and its movements became even more violent with frustration for not being able to throw Luke. It was now extremely angry and was lurching and lunging wildly. Sweat was spraying around from Luke's soaking wet face and hair and a dark patch of sweat was making his shirt stick to his back. Now Wayne felt the temptation to step in and try to bring the furious beast to bear. But as he stepped down from the fence to try and articulate a way how he was going to approach the fray, the horse slowly but surely began to tire. Luke's shocks from the bucking and whiplash slinging slowly became less pronounced. Finally the horse began to visibly slow down until it was brought to a disgruntled trot around the parameters of the pens. Wayne could not conceal his delight and was openly swelling with pride when he laughed and shouted to Luke,

"That's all I wanted from yah Luke, that's all I wanted…Yah can break any hoss yah want now…You've lost yah fear of them at last, at last!"

Luke made sure that the horse was not going to try and throw again and kept on riding round in circles for a few minutes. When he finally pulled the horse to a halt in front of Wayne, he just grinned at him, with his face and hair soaked in sweat.

CHAPTER 12

A boy, a torch and a barn.

Wayne had not slept well again, but this time it was not pleasant thoughts of Belinda that had denied him sleep. He had been dragged from a light slumber by one of his most frequent nightmares and by far the worst. A nightmare of real and phantom spectres, which had come to haunt and taunt him, leaving unanswered questions, echoing around inside of his head. Where do we go when we die? Or do we really ever die? Or is their nothing but oblivion after our lives of pain, joy, happiness and sadness?

It had crept into his slumber in its usual stealth like manner. He was at the Chancellorsville battle again and they had been marching all night. There were twenty six thousand of them moving in block right across the front of the union lines. General Lee had masked their movements by planting another twenty five thousand in battle lines between them and the union lines, which were preparing to be attacked. Nobody had any idea of what General Jackson and General Lee had been planning. But rumours were flying around alarmingly, that General Hooker had deftly shifted a hundred and twenty thousand Federals, complete with artillery across the Rappahannock and Rapidan rivers, twenty-five miles up on the north west of Fredericksburg. And was planning to crush Lee's army of around sixty two thousand in a flank and rear action.

Indeed, Hooker's plan had been so brilliantly executed in the initial movement that he had managed to screen the entire move using cavalry, without Lee being remotely aware that he was about to be attacked from the rear. When he did realise, sudden and precise orders were given all around and with the exception of General Early with ten thousand men under his command, the entire army marched out from their trenches and fieldworks, skirting the heights of Fredericksburg. Of all the battles, which Wayne had great reservations about, this was by far the most depressing.

Where on earth was General Jackson leading them in this forced march, in the pitch dark, through dense and uneven woodlands. Only when the battles lines were finally drawn, would Wayne and all of the boys see the two Generals surprising plans, with great clarity.

They had swung around on the extreme right flank of the Federal army, the whole twenty six thousand of them. Far away and below Wayne could hear the initial cannon and musket fire as Lee and Hooker probed around, feeling each other out, before the full storm of battle erupted. He had been crouching down in some undergrowth, trying to gauge the position and strength of the Federal flank below, situated in the dense forest. Suddenly orders had begun to fly around to fall into battle formations and sweep down onto the Federals in block. Wayne had fallen in with the rest of the exhausted and bewildered boys and away they went. The crunch and muffled thudding through brush and bracken of twenty six thousand veteran soldiers descending on an unaware and exposed left flank of around eight thousand had been the spectral sound, which had been sounding and sifting through Wayne's subconscious mind as an opening to the nightmare in the first place. And the nightmares it panned out into mixed and jumbled pieces had been a nightmare of real events, experienced by real people.

By the time the Federals realised they were being jumped on their right flank, it was too late. Because the thunder of massed musketry and the rebel yell was the first thing they heard, before they could even see anything through the dense and dark trees. The element of surprise had worked better than General Jackson could have anticipated, and shocked Federal officers were desperately trying to turn their companies around to form some semblance of a battle formation, to repulse the descending rebels. The ground before them was so steep that Wayne's boys had to lean backwards as they all advanced.

Wayne could see that the boys who were moving down with him on either side were also having difficulty not falling forward, as they swept down through the trees and undergrowth.

Wayne was on the extreme left flank of a semi circle formation that was about to envelope and crush the Federal right flank. Below them the Federals were trying to turn to face the descending rebels and Wayne could see them moving about through the trees. The first portions to come into close combat were the centre and right flanks of the formation firing down onto the startled Federals, who were still trying to comprehend the full gravity of twenty six thousand armed men moving down onto their positions. Wayne's division was coming down and around the rear of the Federal lines, firing downwards. The rest of the formation had panned out onto more level ground and was lying on a thunderous fire straight into the Federals teetering and disorganised lines. The Federals directly below Wayne were at an even worse disadvantage than the rest, because they were stuck in a depression in the woods and Wayne's division was firing down onto the tops and sides of their heads. And even when they faced upwards to fire, they were being hit in the face and chest by a rain of murderous mass fire.

Wayne and the rest of the boys were now having to jump over the dead and wounded as they came sweeping down and around the depression. The remainder of the Federal lines was breaking up and being pushed up the other side of the depression, only to step right back into another rebel line of battle. The pincer movement was being pressed home with staggering effect and the Federal lines were being squeezed in like a gigantic physical concertina, as General Lee held the front fast, while Stonewall Jackson pressed and squeezed it. But the only song coming from this instrument of death, were the cries of the wounded and panic-stricken men in its deadly grasp.

Wayne was casting his head around and trying to get his bearings, only to see his comrades being felled by musket fire as the Federals came charging back down into the depression with massed Confederates pursuing them from behind. The Federals were massacred were they stood, with no line of escape and heavy fire coming in on them from every angle. This portion of the battle was over now and the remainder of the Union soldiers were throwing down their muskets and surrendering. But there were still a lot of them wandering aimlessly around.

They were dead on their feet; every one of them had been killed instantly by a musket ball or two in the head. Wayne had seen this horrible phenomenon before from other engagements, but nothing on this scale. There were literally dozens of them, passing by and walking into each other. It was as if they were dead, but did not know they were dead and were wandering around, waiting for somebody to break the news to them, so they could drop down dead. Because their spirits had been barbarically removed from their bodies. Wayne watched in morbid fascination as some of his comrades roped off areas of the woods to stop these mechanical spectres crashing into the living. Suddenly the face of one of them was leering straight into his own, he had been a boy of perhaps sixteen. Wayne felt as though somebody had thrust a life-like mannequin from a shop window violently into his arms. And through the boys bare teeth and taut lips, that were curled back in the grimace of sudden death he could hear a shrill, heart wrenching voice imploring him,

'Why did you kill me? Why did you kill me? Why, why, why?'

He was woken up by the sound of his own screaming, which wrenched him from his sleep. He sat bolt upright in his bunk and realised with great relief that he had been dreaming again. His eyes slowly focused on a puzzled and somewhat alarmed Luke, who was holding a cup of coffee out to him. He took the coffee, put it down onto the table and hugged Luke with all his might. But the face of the dead Union boy was still flashing through his mind. After all, he was probably just like Luke.

As they walked over to the stables Wayne suddenly remembered that he wanted to ask Luke something. Luke could sense it and tried to change the anticipated subject.

"Wayne, do yah really think we're losin' the war?"

"We're losin' okay, I really don't know how we've held out for this long."

"That's too bad. Whatyuh gonna do when it's all over?"

Wayne knew that Luke was trying to avoid the pending subject and said casually,

"Where were yah yesterday mornin' Luke? I was lookin' for yah."

"I had things to tend to Wayne, which I couldn't leave."

"You've always told me in the past Luke, when yah needed to do somethin', now tell me the truth. Could it be somethin' to do with the militia passin' through the other mornin'? You know better than to try and bluff me Luke. Now tell me the truth."

Luke drew in a deep breath, released it heavily and turned to Wayne to speak.

"Well, I know you've been good to me Wayne, but if I tell yah, I'll be at yah mercy."

"Go on Luke, I'm listenin.'"

"I've always avoided talkin' 'bout my past Wayne, but you know I trust you."

"Go on Luke, I'm listenin.'"

"I'm wanted for murder."

"What?"

"Yes Wayne, I'm wanted for mass murder."

"Carry on Luke, I'm listenin.'"

"Try to understand Wayne. My family were poor farmers. We had our farm, which mah and pah sacrificed everything to build, in the middle of the Shenandoah Valley, between Cedar creek and Strasburg. We were Quakers and all we ever wanted was peace. Peace for us and everybody else. Our real problems began when my older brother Martin joined the Union army. My pah was a secret union sympathiser and resented the rebel armies robbin' us of our wheat, our sheep, our cows, everythin', as they passed up and down the valley. We could barely feed ourselves in the end, let alone barter anythin'. Well it got far worse when the Union armies under Sheridan moved up the valley, burnin' and destroyin' everythin' they could. I hated them and when my brother got killed at Gettysburg my pah never forgave himself. There was a terrible battle at Cedar creek between General Sheridan and General Early. My pah was a broken man when some of Wade Hampton's cavalry came to rob us of the bare supplies we had to last us through the winter, that the union soldiers had left us.

Well, as seven or eight of them went into our barn to take all we had, I set fire to it, by piling straw in the door and throwin' burnin' torches inside...I killed all of them. But I didn't know that mah pah had hidden six Union boys inside the barn that had been cut off from their regiments during the battle. A Federal Colonel who had tried to find a way back to the union lines had come back to collect them, and I only found out they were in there when he told me. He drew his sword to kill me, so I blew his head off with a shotgun and threw his body in the flames. I had to escape real fast, coz both Federal and rebel soldiers were after me. I nearly got caught by a Federal patrol, but I managed to creep around their camp and put a match to a couple of ammunition wagons to create a diversion and make them think they were being bushwhacked from behind. I blew the camp sky high, killin' a lot more. Win or lose, I ain't got nowhere to go and nothin' to lose Wayne. This war and the whole damn madness of it, means nothin' to me."

"Wow, so you're tellin' me yah torched a barn, killin' six Yankees and eight rebs. Then torched some ammunition wagons, blowing a Federal camp sky high. Why, you sure like matches Luke and you sure picked a fine time to tell me about your talent."

"Well, you did ask my Wayne," answered Luke sheepishly.

CHAPTER 13

This afternoon they had walked a lot further than they usually did, passing the narrow bottleneck of the river, which ran for over two miles. Now they were sitting on the grassy banks, where the river gaped into a wide turbulent body of water. She had her head on his shoulder and appeared to be dozing, with a smile on her face. Wayne was looking out over the vast expanse of dark blue water, to the distant light blue mountains, that appeared to be suspended in mid air on top of a halo of white cloud.

"What are yah thinking Wayne?"

He looked down, kissed her on the top of her head and said,

"Open yah eyes."

As she opened them, Wayne noticed her eyelashes were long and curled upwards.

"What do yah see?"

"I see a river, a blue sky, some high mountains and a lot of trees. What do you see?"

"I see all of those things, but a lot more. I see and feel a, well I mean, I think."

Now she was smiling and nestled her head into his chest."

"What do yah see and feel Wayne? Tell me."

"Well, it's hard to explain, but ever since I was young I had this, what's the word I'm lookin' for, this kinda, kinda hunger, no desire, no kinda instinct. That's the word I'm lookin' for. This kinda instinct to always go and see what's over that next mountain, what's on the other side of that forest, or over those hills. And I just realised I still got those feelings when I look out over the river, among other feelings, among others."

She pressed and nuzzled her head deeper into his chest, smiled broadly, as if she could sense exactly what these other kinda instincts or feelings were and said,

"What are those other feelings, or kinda instincts Wayne?"

Now it was his turn to smile, but he soon slipped into a mode of deeper reflection.

"I've been wonderin' well what I mean is, for some reason, I don't know why, but I damn well wish I'd thought about it while he was still alive. Maybe Wyatt had those same feelings, or desires, only he found them by reading books. I think that maybe his, his hidden, I mean, his kinda blind longings, lived in his books."

"My father used to use the words horizons, horizons to describe those feelings that you're getting at Wayne. And I think you're probably right. That's why he and Joshua would sit me on their laps, even when I was a gal of two and read to me. And when I was 'bout five I was put into school with all the white children. So I could learn, think for myself and appreciate that feeling, that longing, yes, that longing to look for those hidden horizons, and just like you I've ever never lost that desire."

"Wow, horizons, never thoughta that word, that really sums the whole meanin' up. I forgot to as yah where's your pah now? Would sure like to meet him."

He realised that he had asked her something, which was so painful that it was hard for her to talk about, when she started to tremble and tears came to her eyes.

"He's dead, dead...He was killed trying to storm Fort Wagner. And Joshua was killed at the Antietam creek battle, under General Burnside. So I've lost the only two people that I've ever loved in my life, so far. I don't like to let folks get too close now coz every time I do, somethin' happens to them."

Wayne did not know what to say and when he did, he was confounded by a mixed feeling of sympathy, perplexity and cold fear.

"I'm so sorry, does anybody else know that your pah was fightin' for the Yankees."

"No, only you, only you. I would not dare tell anybody else."

"Well please yah don't tell anybody, not even Luke. That lil fella's bin givin' me a few shocks of his own. I'm gonna have to think what I'm gonna do with him."

Wayne was still taking in the panoramic view and contemplating what Belinda had just told him. Now he had two to watch out for, Belinda and Luke. Then he spoke,

"What is real mystery to me, well I mean... Folks like you that study the bible, well how can yah keep on believin'? When so many bad things happen to yah and folks that yah love. I just can't understand how yah can keep on believin'."

"I've never stopped believin'... Oh I've always had doubts, but those were all swept aside when just after my nineteenth birthday my father told me a story about himself and Joshua I will never, ever forget. We were owned by one of the biggest plantation owners in South Carolina named Bertrand Tanner. And unfortunately for us, his slaves and most other folks that had dealin's with him, he was the most brutal and merciless plantation owner in the area. But what I never knew, but always wondered was, why Mister Tanner always left my father alone. Everything fell into place like a big sublime picture as he told me the truth. And he always believed that it was an act of God… And I've always found no other answer, no matter how hard I reflect on it, even now."

Wayne had become intrigued and his attention galvanised as he said,

"This Mister Tanner sounds to be like the big plantation owner in our state called Ben Boucher, didn't think there could be a man more brutal than ole Ben Boucher."

"Oh, I can't speak for Ben Boucher Wayne, but Bertrand Tanner was a man that my father had no reservations 'bout usin' one word he couldn't use on anybody else. And that word was evil, pure, unadulterated evil incarnate, he would call it."

"He sure musta been a real mean dude for yah pah to find fancy words like that to describe him. Thought ole Ben Boucher could have no rival, the way he was."

"Yah ask me how I keep on believin', well I'm gonna tell yah. When yah stop believin' in anythin' at all, then life don't mean nothin'. When yah tell me yah still look out over to the mountains, hills and forests and still have an insatiable desire to know what's on the other side, then you still believe in somethin', somethin', however deep. Yah only have to worry when, or if yah lose that insatiable desire."

"Wow, insatiable desires! I wish you'd stop usin' fancy words Belinda."

"Joshua was the only child of Mary and Bertrand Tanner and she nearly died giving birth to him. He was born on the same day as my father and from a very young age as they grew up together, a deep bond developed between them and that bond never died. Mary was not suited to be a mother and in truth she simply did not know how to be. So my grandmother brought him up mostly, and he spent most of his time around her apron strings, with my father. Problems started when Joshua became of school age and he fretted real badly, being separated from my grandmother and my father. This is when my father saw brutality for the first time, because Mister Tanner would beat Joshua without mercy. My father told me that this would hurt him more than Joshua and he dreaded Mister Tanner coming to collect him. But because Mary was completely incapable of taking care of Joshua, he still spent all of his time out of school with my grandmother and my father. It was the only love he knew and all he wanted was to be with them. My father would go down to the school and wait for Joshua to come out each afternoon. He would listen at the school window and wished he could be inside with Joshua. One day the schoolmistress came out amongst the children and noticed my father waiting by the gate. When she asked him who he was waiting for, he replied my friend Joshua. Joshua appeared and took my father by the hand and said to the puzzled schoolmistress, 'this is my friend Moses and he wants to be in school with me, but he's not allowed.' Her reply was, 'Do you really want to go to school to learn like Joshua Moses?'

His reply was, 'yes ma'am I do, I do really wanna learn.'

She then slipped into a mood of deep reflection, as if she was speaking through the voice of her father. Wayne slowly discovered the reasons why she was so articulate.

"So this ageing school Ma'am let my father sit outside the window on a chair, which she passed through and gave him a pencil and paper, or sometimes a chalk-board with chalk and the window ledge became his desk. He had such fond memories of this woman, because what she was doing was completely unorthodox and could of got her into serious trouble. But when she realised that my father was learning very quickly and was eager to learn, she would give him extra work to do at home. He would have to creep away and leave over the back fence of the school when the school bell rang. That was his warning bell that some parents would be waiting at the school gate for their children to come out, and he dare not be seen for his sake and the teachers. Luckily the other children accepted this, although most of them found it strange why he should be sitting outside. He would wait for Joshua down the road and pounce on him from out of the hedgerows. As I told you, that bond never died and as Mister Tanner became aware of it as they grew closer together, not only did he try to break it, but teach Joshua in the art of cruelty and brutality. Mister Tanner was very fond of using his whip on anybody, for any reason. He was even notorious to other plantation owners in the area for his love of it. And my father would say that the use and administration of it as he damn well pleased, was the outlet where he relieved his greatest pleasures. When he told me this I didn't realise that he meant warped sexual pleasure, but that's another story… Mister Tanner grew to hate Mary, because of her interest in Joshua and his progression on the path to being a man, or rather brute, was not materialising as he had planned. In truth Mary was not much more than a soulless wretch, completely void of feelings, other than her own few comforts… Now when Mister Tanner's temper got out of control, which was quite frequent, he would haul a handful of slaves out to one of the barns to whip them, for no reason… This is where Joshua learnt to hate his father with a vengeance. A hatred that smouldered and grew in silent brooding suffering…

Mister Tanner had a hireling called Lyle that would do anything that Mister Tanner told him to do. When the slave's backs were bare and they were bracing themselves to be whipped, Lyle would stand by with a shotgun, gloating… After he had whipped the slaves until he was adequately satisfied, he would hand Joshua the whip and tell him to prove that he was a man. Joshua would tremble and cry, but would feign weakness as he wielded the whip as gently as he could… Mister Tanner would snatch the whip out of his hand in anger and frustration and show him how it was done, with relish… He would then grab my father, rip his shirt off and thrust the whip into Joshua's hand and say to him, 'now show your friend who is master.' Joshua could not raise his hand to my father, so again Mister Tanner would show him how it was done. He would hand Joshua the whip again and say, 'now show your friend who is master.' Still Joshua could not strike my father's back and his hands would drop. Then Mister Tanner would completely go berserk and rip Joshua's shirt off and whip him so viciously that my father would try to grab the whip from his hand, only to receive the same punishment. It would be worse when Mister Tanner had been at the whisky. And worse still when he had argued with Mary, calling her a morose, worthless trollop and then hit the bottle. They were nine years old and already the bond was growing strong… When they entered their teens they would spend from sun up to sundown on long fishin' trips, or just livin' out in the wild. That was before my father was forced to workin' long hours in the cotton fields. Even then Joshua would come out to visit him. They would share secrets and I think that even from this age my father knew the truth about Joshua."

Wayne interrupted her and she appeared to be woken from a trance-like daze.

"What was the truth 'bout Joshua?"

She just smiled and carried on with the story, reverting back to her trance-like state.

"Well, Joshua was very handsome. Tall, with golden curly hair and green piercing eyes. The gals would go wild when they saw him and as luck would have it, which was unfortunate luck for Joshua, a daughter of another very rich plantation owner took a real shinin' to Joshua. Joshua would have been about eighteen by now and most of the wealthy plantation boys and even poor boys were becoming interested in gals. Mister Tanner of course was thoroughly delighted that the gal of another rich plantation owner should be interested in Joshua and laid out plans and invites to dinner, so they could get to know each other. Well this is how my father met my mother. She would come out to the plantation as an escort for the gal. My mother was very beautiful and for my father it was love at first sight. So the gal was very pretty, but Joshua just was not interested in her. Even now Mister Tanner who was by now heavily addicted to whisky couldn't understand why Joshua was extremely reluctant to entertain the gal."

"Why wasn't Joshua interested in the gal?" asked Wayne, looking puzzled.

Belinda could not hide her own amusement when she replied.

"Well, some gentlemen don't like gals Wayne, don't you know that?"

Wayne became slightly embarrassed, because he thought that she was mocking him.

"Why sure I know that, I just don't meet many such gentlemen."

This made her giggle and Wayne became more embarrassed about his ignorance on matters he did not understand. Belinda looked at him like a concerned mother.

"Well, it took a while but romance between my father and mother blossomed at these meetings, but for Joshua it became a living nightmare. Even when Mister Tanner arranged meetings with other wealthy plantation owner's daughters, which fell flat every time; Mister Tanner could not understand the reason why. My father reasoned that the whisky by now had taken over a large part of Mister Tanner's life and he was becoming apathetic.

My mother gradually became accepted by Joshua and she became friendly with him, but it took some coaxing. I think she suspected his relationship with my father was rather strange and may have had a sexual connotation. But she soon learned that their friendship was platonic and my father of course proved his sexual persuasions without any doubt… My father's desire to learn never lost its passion and Joshua would smuggle books and dictionaries from his father's library and my father would eagerly study them. He would take words from the dictionary and study the meanings from every aspect, so he could apply those words in conversation. He was becoming very well educated right under Mister Tanner's nose, by Mister Tanner's books and he never suspected it… He would, and it would be under bizarre circumstances. I was born on the plantation, delivered by my grandmother. My grandmother who had delivered so many children from other plantations told my father that this gal is special… She has the beauty of her mother and the mind of her father. My father was very keen for me to learn from a very young age and he was always trying to pass knowledge on to me… When I was about two disaster struck. A fever so bad and so deadly struck the area. My mother died and so did many others on her plantation, includin' the owner and two of his children. Incredibly the Tanner place was untouched by it and I was quickly sent to stay with my father. This is how my relationship developed with Joshua, he took the place of my mother... Mister Tanner's behaviour did not change, in fact it got worse and his hatred for Mary and Joshua became borderin' on manic. The death of my mother affected my father very badly, but it did not prevent him from learnin'. And Joshua would keep smuggling books to him from the big old house."

Wayne could feel the sense of deep sadness in her voice now. But the picture about her was becoming as big and panoramic as the one that was facing them. As vast and breathtaking as the mountains, rivers and endless blue skies that filled the heart with wonder. She was far from finished and her voice became all pervading to Wayne's senses. Carrying him away on flight of sheer incredulity and marvel.

"On the bend of a road in South Carolina is a tall and ancient oak tree. Deep in the bark of that tree is carved the names, Joshua and Moses... Friends forever. This was the place where my father believed from the bottom of his heart that God came down from heaven to try and test him. To put into his hands the tools for either revenge or redemption. I would have been about a gal of two at the time and my father kept the secret for all of those years, because that secret belonged to him and Joshua alone. On one side of that bend lies cotton fields, Tanner's cotton fields, high up from the road. But on the other side, in the crook of the bend is a low laying mire of quicksand, directly beneath that tree... It had been a hot summer's day and my father had been put to work by Mister Tanner in that corner of a field, not far from the tree. My father had come back late afternoon to the slave quarters and realised that he had left some tools close to where he and been workin' and he had to go back for them... Just as he was about to pick the tools up, he heard a horse approaching on the road below. He was vaguely aware of the bend in the road, but couldn't see it from where he was. The horse could clearly be heard being pressed at full gallop, when suddenly there was a shriek of terror from the horse and a thunder of jumping hooves, as the horse threw its rider. My father immediately thought that some wild animal had ran out in front of the horse and caused the horse to throw its occupant... So he walked over to the corner of the field, looked over the hedge and saw none other than Mister Bertrand Tanner stuck knee deep in the quicksand. The horse had thrown him so forcefully that he had landed a good ten feet out into the mire and he was slowly sinking. My father climbed over the hedge, down onto the road and tried to gather his thoughts... The first thing Mister Tanner shouted when seeing my father was, 'Quick, pull me outa here Moses, or I'll whip yah so bad, yah won't be able to lay down for weeks.' A cold, calculating calm came over my father as if somebody or somethin' was guidin' him... He just calmed the horse, stroked Mister Tanner's hound dog, sat down on a stump and looked down onto the helpless Mister Tanner...

Mister Tanner could not contain his rage on seeing my father's antics and bawled at him, 'Git that rope off ma horse and pull me outa here now Moses, or I'll break my whip on yah back, damn you!' My father just sat there watchin', as Mister Tanner slowly sank into the mire, throwing every curse, every threat and message of doom that he could... He only became aware of his own plight when my father just smiled on him and said, 'So you're gonna damn me, whip me and punish me with all the hell and damnation you can Mister Tanner.' But even now Mister Tanner could not comprehend that he was in deadly trouble and completely at the mercy of my father. 'I'm warnin' yah Moses you're gonna pay for this, damn you,' would be the last threat that he would ever make to my father... Eventually Mister Tanner was forced into taking a more conciliatory tone as it slowly dawned on him that he was at the complete and utter mercy of my father. 'Come on Moses, all yah gotta do is git that rope off ma horse, throw it out to me and tie it to the horse and I'll be clear, come on Moses.' By this time Mister Tanner was nearly up to his waist in the mire and had become horribly aware that his movements were pulling him down more quickly. He stopped movin' and looked up at my father for the first time... Now my father knew that it was his turn to speak and Mister Tanner became perplexed and very afraid...

'Well, well Mister Tanner... Who can you call to get you outa this mess? Er, what's your attorney's name? Mister Birtles! Ah, yes, yes Mister Birtles I believe. The same Mister Birtles who you instruct to find a clause, or exercise his power of attorney to swindle some poor smallholder farmer out of his land and property. Or to pay him a pittance, which your attorney can find a clause in the contract, which you apply yourself, so he forgoes any payment. Or maybe Mister Birtles can study his law books and find some legally binding paragraph, that can save you from death...Oh Mister Tanner, I see you're lookin' at me in astonishment. You cannot believe I understand your skulduggery with Mister Birtles. Mister Tanner was indeed completely surprised and stunned as my father spoke to him, using words and grammar that he didn't know my father could ever possess.

Well, Mister Tanner, from what I gather from the last time I was listening at your window, the bad news is that Mister Birtles is away on business over in Atlanta so that counts him out. No clause or reprieve can be applied… Oh Mister Tanner, who else can we bring as a witness in your trial? Oh yes! The Reverend Archibald Dinwiddie, who you have long conversations in religion and theology with… Perhaps there's somethin' in his books, some theory, or biblical story that may compare to your fate… But there again of course, the good Reverend Dinwiddie would never know that you would tie me up and sodomise me when I was only eight years old… Was it the whisky that compelled you to sodomise me? After you had just beaten your wife… No, no, no, because you didn't even need that demon as an excuse to sodomize me, once you became accustomed to your own lust… Well, now what, now what Mister Tanner? Your poor horse cannot reason and he threw you so high in the air when he got scared, that he can't be used as a reliable witness. Well, what about Rusty, your good ole faithful hound dog who you whip even when he gives you affection. The poor ole boy can't reason to go and get help for yah. By now Mister Tanner was up to his chest in the mire and it would have been very hard to pull him out, but my father was still torn between saving him or lettin' him die. And as Mister Tanner realised that he was about to die he began to plead with my father and beg for his life. 'Please Moses, I'm sorry 'bout anythin' I did to yah. Do yah want yah freedom? I'll give yah yah freedom… Money, I'll give yah money and yah freedom. Please Moses, pull me outa here, I give yah ma word I won't ever raise mah hand to yah agin. Please Moses, show some compassion for a man about to die.' My father just said, 'compassion, you dare to use the word compassion at your own trial. Well, I think that's what's called using false evidence, or bearing false witness, dependin' if you're speakin' in legal terms, or religious terms. But I'm afraid the trial is outa my hands now Mister Tanner, because Joshua has been implicated. It was Joshua who lent me your books to educate myself… Your own books gave me the means to think, reason and apply the knowledge, which I have and cherish…

I often wondered if we read the same books Mister Tanner, judging by our differences… No, I cannot risk you punishing and taking reprisals on Joshua… Because Joshua is a far greater man than you could ever be Mister Tanner. You may use a whip on another man's back, without mercy, or pity… But your own son Joshua can feel that whip on another man's back. He can feel every single lash as if that bloody and broken back was his own. Well Mister Tanner, all the evidence has been presented and your trial is coming to an end. I am your judge and jury… How do you plead? Guilty, or not guilty.' By now Mister Tanner had resided himself to the fact that my father was surely about to let him die, but he tried one last plea of mercy, before the mire dragged him under… 'Moses, I promise yah if I can't give yah freedom, or money, what in the name of God can I do for you to show me mercy? You have my word, I won't punish Joshua, or you, please, please…!

My father had achieved what he had been aiming for right from the opening minutes of finding Mister Tanner stuck in the quicksand. But he needed to be completely sure that he didn't go back on his word. So he still let Mister Tanner think that he was going to die. 'Now it's Friday, so Lyle be up in town, drinkin' and gamblin' his wages around the saloons. That means he won't be back 'til the early hours and he won't notice your absence until 'bout mid day, when he comes over to the house… That means, when I take your hoss and dog, nobody will know, or ever find out what happened to yah Mister Tanner… I find you guilty Mister Tanner and I as your judge, jury and finally your executioner, hereby sentence you to death, death Mister Tanner.' With that he began to walk away, leaving Mister Tanner weeping in the mire… But then at the last moment he turned around and said, 'Oh yes, there is one thing that can give you a reprieve, and I almost forgot Mister Tanner.'

'What is it Moses? I'll give you exactly what you want.' My father just pulled a rope and a whip from the horse and held them up and said, 'in my right hand I have a whip, which can only be used to maim, mutilate, hurt and scar. But in my left hand I hold a rope, which can be used to tie and enslave, to bind and bond innocent people…

Or it can be used to release from bondage and to rescue, lift up and pull free. The question for you Mister Tanner is how do I use this rope? Do you really believe I should pull you free? All I want from you is one thing Mister Tanner, not money, or freedom. Those things can eventually be had with what I want from you.' Mister Tanner was by now so desperate to save himself he just pleaded with my father…'Anythin' you want Moses anythin', but please have mercy on me.'

My father finally believed that Mister Tanner was being truthful.

'My gal Belinda is only two years old. All I want from, you Mister Tanner, is for you to use your influence to put her into school, so that she can learn to read and write like all of the white children… That's all I want from you…'

'You have your wish Moses, you have my word.' With that my father threw him the rope, tied it to the horse and pulled Mister Tanner free… Joshua listened in disbelief when my father told him what had happened and asked him why he just didn't let die… My father could not give him a certain answer, but he'd felt that he was being guided by somebody, or somethin'. So I went to school and my father would give me words and make me study each words meaning from every aspect. By the time war broke out Mister Tanner was a wreck, the whisky had finally got the better of him. It was beneath that tree that my father and Joshua said their last goodbyes, before going to join the union armies. They had both been oppressed in different ways and they had suffered their separate oppression together. And they both sincerely believed that a new and bright beginning was about to free all oppressed and disenfranchised people. They promised that they would meet there again, under that old oak tree when the war was over. My father went to join General Hinks and Joshua, General Burnside. They never came back… I used to go and visit that spot every day and I swear that I can feel their presence, I just know that they are there with me, I can feel them…'

She put her head into Wayne's chest and began to cry, with her whole body trembling. Wayne gently stroked her hair and pulled her close to him. He couldn't find the words to express his sympathy, so he just looked out over the river and mountains, with every fibre of his being torn asunder.

CHAPTER 14

Luke was grooming a slim and athletic brown horse with white markings as Belinda approached. Luke was well aware of the friendship between Belinda and Wayne and in a vague sort of way he appreciated it, because she obviously had a calming effect on Wayne's volatile temper. Although Wayne's tirades against him had diminished to only the occasional reprimand for not listening to his instructions properly, Luke had noticed a marked change in Wayne's character.

"Hi, Luke, is Wayne about?" she asked.

"Hi, Belinda, Wayne's not here, I thought he was with you."

"No, I left him by the well 'bout an hour ago."

"Can't tell you where he is now, I don't ask him too much," said Luke.

"Don't worry, I think I know where he is… Sure is a fine looking gal," said Belinda, patting the horse's back affectionately.

"She sure is, a little wild still, but Wayne's let me work on her alone."

Belinda just smiled and said, "I'm sure you're doin' a fine job Luke."

Luke became slightly embarrassed, a beautiful woman had never spoken to him in his life before, let alone pay him a compliment.

"Mind if I see how she handles," she said.

Luke became visibly uncomfortable on hearing this and said,

"Wow, well I'd sure let yah Belinda, but as I said she's still a little wild… Wayne would go crazy if yah had an accident and he'd blame me."

"Don't fret Luke, I've bin ridin' horses since I was a gal of six. I was brought up with them, I'm sure you're doin' a fine job on her."

"Well okay Belinda, but I don't want any trouble from Wayne, he can have a mean temper when somebody crosses him."

Then much to Luke's surprise Belinda casually swung herself up onto the horse in one athletic sweep and nudged the surprised horse into a canter with her bare feet.

"Be careful, she ain't got no saddle on and she can move real fast!" shouted Luke.

But he just stood and watched in awe with his mouth open as Belinda pushed the horse into an easy and well-controlled gallop around the parameters of the pens. Eventually she pulled the horse up beside Luke and swung down from its back as casually as she had mounted it… She handed Luke the reins and said,

"Well, you sure have done a fine job on her Luke, as I just found out."

Luke tried to give the appearance of being serious, but inside he was swelling with pride. He would tell Wayne anyway, even if Belinda didn't. He had been surprised by the way Wayne had responded when he had told him about his chequered past. Murder was not something anybody could take lightly, let alone mass murder. But Wayne had been almost sympathetic in his manner. Luke reasoned that maybe a man who had seen so much killing and had killed himself, had possibly become immune to death and killing. The big question for him is where did he go when all of this was over. Wayne had been an unlikely friend, confidant and ultimately a surrogate father.

The war was virtually lost, and around camp the very atmosphere smelt of defeat. But nobody wanted to talk about it. Because nobody knew if that defeat would come down in murderous, revengeful hammer blows, or a peaceful signing and passing of documents. Either way, Luke knew that if the truth about himself was recognised, he would surely be treated like a murdering bushwhacker by either side. He could not ask any more from Wayne, but the cold fact was that Wayne was all he had. This strange, lonely man had given him a chance and he wanted to stay with him.

At the same time Luke was gawping at Belinda's apparent expertise at horse handling, Jed Wallace was looking out over the dusty square, through a dusty window. Jed was a man with a mission and he had been planning and scheming the execution of that mission for sometime. And his quarry was about to come off duty from the old jailhouse where he had been guarding, or abusing the latest bunch of Yankee prisoners, which were about to be transported south. It was ironic that Jed never wanted to fight in the first place, but circumstances had dragged him into the confederate army.

At one stage he thought that the war might pass him by completely, and in his shrewd and wise old head, he never really believed it could be won by the south. The ranch where he had worked for years was perched up on a plateau, surrounded by lush green fields, watered by streams that spiralled down from the Tennessee mountains. He would watch the grey clad confederate armies far down below, moving north along the winding valley roads and speculate how long it would take for them to come back. Blundering along down the same roads, with their numbers, artillery pieces and supply wagons seriously depleted. The northern invader was making inroads deep into western territories. Firstly through Kansas, Missouri and Kentucky, states, which harboured people with mixed loyalties. Now they were probing across and down into Tennessee, with the Tennessee river as a very handy means of mass transportation for the union armies. Jed knew that it was only a question of time, when the terrible battle at Shiloh church happened only a few miles away. When it had erupted Jed had thought that Albert Sidney Johnston's army was still in camp at Corinth, just over the other side of the mountains. He only became aware that something dramatic was happening, when he heard the dull rhythmic thud of massed artillery vibrating through the ether. And the next day the telltale mark of a defeated army, shambling back along the roads, with the wounded and dying laying pell-mell and piled up in the back of ambulance wagons.

The day the union army overran the ranch, Jed had been branding cattle in one of the barns. As he worked he could hear the familiar rumble of cavalry, marching men and the crunch of artillery wheels on stone, but this time it was extremely close. Cold fear crept up his spine, when he heard the sound of fencing and posts being smashed and broken up and frightened cattle being herded up. When he walked over to look out of the barn door he saw that the union army had arrived in force. Mounted Officers were barking orders to tired and irritable blue clad soldiers. There were thousands of them and they were swarming over the whole ranch. They had not come up from the valley roads, they had come up over the mountains, and descended on the ranch through a hardly used and isolated road.

Jed had been totally powerless, along with the owner of the ranch and the two other ranch hands to stop the union soldiers dismantling and taking anything they could make use of. He had watched the northern boys with guarded interest. They didn't look any different from the southern boys, only their uniforms were blue and they looked slightly better fed. But what had struck him the most was the sheer array of equipment and supplies. Cavalry, with Spencer repeater carbines, perched on well-fed horses. At least twenty-five artillery pieces complete with full ammunition wagons. And last of all the infantry, with their muskets and knapsacks, milling about in their thousands. It was difficult to believe that the far more sparsely equipped confederate armies had been fending off and in some cases, defeating military might on this scale. When they had finished their almost clinical stripping of the ranch, like locusts on a ripe crop, they just casually fell into formations and streamed down onto the valley roads far below. Jed had walked over to the owner, Mister John Cunningham who was just standing holding one of his J.C. branding irons in disbelief and told him,

"Well it looks like I gotta go and fight now Mister C.

What Jed had detested most about the war was, it was always the innocent that had suffered the most. Whether it was a man like Mister Cunningham, who only wanted to be left alone to make a living. Or a boy of sixteen, laying dead in his arms, with his bare feet swinging around as Jed carried him over to a mass grave and rudely dumped in with confederate and union boys. For a man that had never wanted to fight, he had been in some of the worse battles. He had been at Stone's river, when General Rosecrans attacked General Braxton Bragg's right flank and General Bragg had attacked General Rosecrans right flank simultaneously. The attack on the confederate right flank and been blunted by Bragg, but much to everybody's surprise including General Bragg, the confederate attack swept right around the union right, flanking them. This was because General Rosecrans had ordered his soldiers to light fires in the night, far out on their right flank, to give the impression that his lines were far longer and fortified on his right.

He had not anticipated that Bragg was about to attack that flank and the decoy backfired badly. Jed had been in the assault and could not believe that when they were ordered to move forward at daybreak, through the cold damp air, that the Federals had not opened fire. This was because there were no Federals. Even when four columns of massed confederates forded the shallow of the streams, swept up onto the high ground and panned out, all they could find were the smouldering cinders of many fires. So they all had to perform a sharp right angle turn, and roll down through an ancient cedar wood. When they eventually came piling out of the wood, they finally found the Federal right flank, at breakfast. Jed could still remember the look of shock on the union boys' faces as they heard the rebel yell, before seeing thousands of rebel soldiers charging out from the trees. They didn't even have time to grab their muskets, or unlimber their artillery pieces before they were chopped down in a hail of massed musketry, men and horses. Jed had joined some boys to unlimber the captured cannons and turn them on the Federals who were fleeing in a wholesale route. Because General

Rosecrans had been forced to re-enforce his right flank urgently, Bragg had managed to buckle in the union left, clasping the whole union army in a spearhead formation. Then for some inexplicable reason Bragg held off for two days, made a half-hearted attack on the union left, which was repulsed by artillery. And then much to the relief of the union Generals pulled away from the battlefield, with both Generals declaring victory.

This was not the only time he had been right in the middle of the peculiar and unpredictable ways of battle. This time it was at Chickamauga and Jed would learn after the battle that it would be the unfortunate union General Crittenden, the same General who was in command of the union right at Stone's river, who would be in the middle of another military blunder. He could clearly remember squatting in a thick and overgrown wood, waiting for the order to charge. He knew that General Longstreet was in command and was piling thousands of boys into the woods and was using the wood as cover, before letting rip with one of his characteristic whiplash attacks with massed infantry.

But what Jed and the boys did not know was that union orders had got mixed up and General Wood who was facing them was given orders to move his troops out of line, march them around the back of General Crittendon's lines who were on General Woods left. Then go and support General Thomas who was being attacked by massed confederates under Generals Polk and Forrest in front of Snodgrass hill.

When General Longstreet gave the order to charge, they had all stormed forward out of the woods, thousands of them crammed together so tightly that Jed was lifted clean off the ground, and squeezed between the shoulders of two burly farm boys. Much to the amazement of everybody, the whiplash attack was not impeded or blunted in any way by musketry, or the dreaded Federal artillery, because there was nobody in front. So the point of that whiplash kept slicing forward, cutting the union army clean in half, like a razor sharp dicing knife. Jed remembered the boys spilling out into the left and right flanks in sheer disbelief. He had been on the left, chasing the panic stricken Federals through the gaps in missionary ridge, while the Federal left was being pursued vigorously by the confederate right, until it was within the lines of General Thomas.

Jed had reflected at the time, that if the union Generals made any more incomprehensible blunders, then the victory that Jed had always reasoned as nigh on impossible was beginning to twinkle like a distant light on the horizon. That light had not come any closer, it had soon faded and died in a series of disasters, all of which Jed had been part of. Firstly came the Federal attack on missionary ridge, where the army of the Cumberland had stormed up from five hundred feet below, from a position where it had been held as virtual prisoners in front of Chattanooga, pulling off one of the most spectacular victories of the war. And Jed could still hear the sound of musket balls whizzing past his ears and the thud of those tiny messengers of death, imbedding themselves deep in the backs of his comrades, as they fled down the other side of the ridge. Then came Franklin, when General Hood ordered a suicidal attack on massed Federal artillery and infantry, planted in two impenetrable semi circles on high ground, overlooking the confederate attack and every single movement that the confederates made.

Then finally for Jed, when General Thomas stormed out of Nashville, completely routing the remainder of Hoods battered army. And Jed could clearly still feel the cold fear of running through the pitch dark and the flashes and snap of carbines as General Wilson's crack cavalry units hunted for them like dogs in the night. This is where Jed had sustained the wound to his eye. He had been hiding behind a tree, when a bullet rebounded down from a branch as he peered around the tree to try and see where the enemy was. The bullet had smashed through his brow and lodged itself just below his eye. He had been found the next morning by Bedford Forrest's cavalry, who had been providing a rear guard. When they realised that he was not dead, they had quickly brought him to a field hospital.

Jed was not bitter about all that he had seen and suffered, only sad. He was bearing a cross of melancholy, that only a man that was a victim of events and circumstances beyond his own control could carry.

He was brought back to reality as the door of the jailhouse opened and a big burly figure stepped out. He quickly rubbed some surplus dust from the window and adjusted his eye patch. He saw all he needed to know. It was Clayton, he was on duty and he would be alone, perfect. Jed quietly muttered to himself, 'Well Clayton, you won't be tellin' any tall stories tonight to the boys, coz yah won't be goin' to the party and you sure won't be goin' up to Petersburg next week.'

Clayton was standing in the porch, with his thumbs hooked in his belt, looking around. He should be relieved in about an hour's time. That would give Jed plenty of time to execute the final stages of his plan. As Clayton turned around and went back through the door, Jed smiled to himself. He was about to kill the only man that he had ever hated in his life. He owed it to the boys, he owed it to the Yankee prisoners and he owed it to the blond, fiery boy Wayne Rawlins.

CHAPTER 15

Wayne was splashing around in the water. It felt good to wash away the sweat and the smell of horses. This was his favourite time of day, with the golden sun reflecting on the clear, slowly running water. Here he could wallow about in peace, reflecting on his deepest and most profound thoughts just like the sun sparkling and reflecting across the water. When he had arrived at the camp, he had no serious responsibilities, other than to take care of himself. But over the past few weeks an obscure, nagging feeling had been lolling about in the back of his mind. And it had grown and slowly presented itself as crystal clear as the pools that lined the edge of the river. He felt responsible not only for Belinda, but Luke as well. With Belinda, there should not be any problems when surrender was imminent. After all, her father had fought and died for their side. But when everybody cleared out to go home, what if the rebel militia found out somehow about Belinda's father? The big question was, would there be bitter reprisals, or brutal vengefulness from a defeated army who could not accept defeat. Now what about Luke? Well he was in a no mans land of his own. He had killed men on both sides in what could easily be deemed as fiendish circumstances by both sides. He was still pondering these thoughts as he stood up in the shallows to walk back to the shore, when suddenly he heard Belinda's voice, loud and clear.

"Oh Wayne, Wayne, I thought I'd find yah here… I'm sure glad you're naked agin."

He quickly tried to cover his manhood with both hands and Belinda burst out laughing.

"Don't bother to try to cover yashelf up Wayne, I've seen yah naked before."

"Belinda, whatyah doin' here? I left yah by the well. Where's mah clothes, where's mah towel?" shouted Wayne while crouching down in the water to hide his nakedness.

Belinda just laughed even louder and said, "I told yah Wayne, I've seen yah stark naked before and I sure like what I see."

"Now this ain't no time to be playin' games Belinda, now where's mah clothes?"

Belinda produced Wayne's clothes and towel from behind her back, made a gesture to hand them to him and then threw them up into the branches of a nearby tree.

"Yah won't be needin' any clothes for a while Wayne," she said in earnest.

Wayne watched her in sheer disbelief and wonder as she casually slipped out of her white robe and spoke to him almost mockingly.

"Well Wayne, do yah like what yah see?"

Wayne didn't even recognise his own voice as he said in amazement,

"I like everythin' I see Belinda, everythin.'"

He stood up and dropped his hands to his sides. He couldn't speak because it was taking all of his senses to take stock and marvel at her incredible beauty. Her breasts were magnificent, with nipples like dark, erect buds. Her waist and stomach were slim and tapered out into shapely hips and strong, lithe legs. After what seemed like an eternity she spoke and her voice made him feel as if his heart was about to explode.

"I want you Wayne, I've wanted you from the moment I met you…It's time Wayne…"

With that she slowly walked down into the water, never taking her eyes off him. She slipped easily into his arms, put her arms around his waist and kissed him. He slid his hands down around her waist and caressed her soft buttocks. She nuzzled her cheek into the side of his neck and he kissed her forehead. Her hands slipped down his back and grasped his buttocks. She pulled him close and her breasts pressed into his upper abdomen, sending shivers down his spine. Any urge to cover his manhood had evaporated and he could feel that manhood growing and expanding. Any feeling of self-consciousness had flown away, because he was in the arms of a woman who loved him. He could feel that she loved him and he loved her in a way, which defied description.

She slipped out of his arms and led him by the hand out into deeper water. She then slipped behind him and climbed up onto his back. He could feel the softness of her loins nestling onto the base of his back and her breasts resting on his shoulders. He then dived forward, taking both of them out and under into the depths. They surfaced and separated, taking each other by the hands like dancers. The current in the centre of the river was quite strong and as they trod water it pulled them around, whirling, twisting and turning them in unison. Both of them were overwhelmed by a deep sense of freedom and wonder. They became swept along into the bottleneck and carried out towards where the river panned out from the trees, into the panoramic circumstance of the mountains. They were still holding hands and being whirled around by the whim and temperament of their watery host when Wayne kicked, pushed and pulled to bring them to the shore. When his feet finally felt the pebbles of the shallows, he swept her up in his arms and carried her to the shore. She was quietly watching his face, as water from his wet hair dripped down onto her breasts and trickled down into her navel, making a small pool before slipping down either side of her stomach. She knew where he was taking her and as he pushed through some bracken and laid her down onto a soft grassy clearing, she knew that the time had come at last. A soft breeze was rapidly drying their bodies and his manhood was becoming hard and erect, as his piercing blue eyes bored into her own. The same manhood that she had seen on her initial discovery whilst stumbling upon him while he was bathing was now in front of her, standing erect and proud, in a bow shaped display of strength. It was now unsheathed and shining like a purple ripe plum and she wondered if she could accommodate it. She could accommodate it, but he was in no rush as he kissed her all over, moving down from her neck, to her breasts, to her stomach and then ultimately to the inside of her legs and loins. They made love in wild abandon, caressing and sliding around together like a living bodily puzzle, trying and finding ways to piece into one. He pushed and probed into every orifice in her body, sending her to heaven. She pushed him onto his back and lowered herself gently on to his throbbing, hot manhood.

She could feel it pulsating with his warm blood deep inside of her. And then the warm discharge of his semen burst into her, transcending every fibre of her being as they climaxed together.

They lay naked, like two innocent children in the Garden of Eden. Her head was resting on his chest and she could hear his heart slowly ticking down into a rhythmic, steady beating. The pleasant smell of his musk was in the air as he gently stroked her face and hair. His hair was now dry and was gently being ruffled like ripe corn in a warm, summer breeze. Belinda deeply wanted this moment to last. Because at last she had found the man who could deliver her from all of her pain and suffering. Her father and Joshua were gone forever. But at the end of her lonely vigil she had found a man by chance, or accident who loved her just as much, or more as they had. Or was it by chance or accident? Were they watching over her, was the question. She could swear that she could feel their presence down by that old oak tree, where her father always believed that he was given the chance for revenge or redemption. And now she could feel their presence again, stronger than ever, as she lay in the arms of this magnificent man. Had they somehow brought him to her? To protect and care for each other.

"Well Wayne, what now? What's on yah mind?"

"You're on mah mind Belinda… You've never bin off mah mind from the time I met yah down by the well. And I don't bleeve I'm ever gonna git yah outa mah mind."

Belinda pulled him close, lifted her head from his chest and kissed him on the mouth.

"That's all I wanted to hear Wayne, that's all I wanted to know," she said.

She then rolled over and straddled him, lowering herself gently onto his manhood.

CHAPTER 16

Jed knocked on the door of the jailhouse and waited. When there was no answer he slowly opened the door and walked in. Clayton was sitting in a wooden chair, with his feet upon the desk. Jed was sorely tempted to kill him there and then as the bile of pure hatred churned and welled up inside his stomach. But no, this man who had never wanted to fight had something to say before he dispatched Clayton from this world. As he turned around to close the door he noticed with delight that Clayton had left the keys in the door. He deftly covered the door and turned the key, making as little noise as possible. Clayton was surprised to see Jed, but not unduly alarmed.

"What do yah want Wallace, yah ole buzzard? Don't yah know this place is outa bounds to everybody except for the boys that do their duties here?"

"Oh I know it's outa bounds Jake, but I may not git another chance to say goodbye, farewell, or adios to yah Jake, now that would be a pity now wouldn't it Jake."

Even now Clayton had not sensed that he was in trouble. After all, what could a wiry old man who was blind in one eye do to him?

"Git to the point Wallace, I git relieved in about half an hour and I don't wanna be seen talkin' with a no good ole buzzard like you Wallace."

"I'm sure you don't Jake, I'm sure you don't. When you're tellin' all those stories to the boys tonight, I'm sure yah don't want them to know I was at most of the battles you talk so grandly about Jake. But ain't it strange I never wanted to fight Jake."

"What are yah implyin' Wallace… If you're callin' me a liar and a coward, I'll…"

"Well I ain't callin' yah anythin' Jake, we both know what yah are Jake…And all of those boys think you're some big, brave hero Jake, now ain't that good for yah Jake."

"Git outa here Wallace, before I blind yah in yah other eye," shouted Clayton.

Jed just chuckled and adjusted his eye patch, then said,

"I remember the first time I saw yah Jake. Just after we tried to burst outa Atlanta and was cut to bits by Federal cannon and musket fire… I was carryin' a boy of maybe sixteen in my arms. Can still remember his bare feet swingin' around and his young face lookin' like he was only sleepin'. I can remember droppin' him in that blood soaked grave with the Federal and reb' boys, some 'bout the same age as him. Then I turn round and see you Jake, no sorry, I heard yah braggin' before I saw yah… Braggin' about your part in the battle Jake…From what I could hear yah would have been in my division, in the very same line as me Jake… Now ain't it strange I never saw yah in the fight Jake, coz you're quite a big fella. Oh Jake, I shoulda known then, coz yah weren't in the battle… Just like you weren't at the Nashville fight, when we were fightin' back to back against the Yankees… Just like you weren't at the Franklin fight when so many boys were killed before they could even move into battle lines. Those boys that sit around that fire at night are sure impressed by the battles that you were never in Jake. Those same boys who really did fight, who really did see their comrades killed and never, ever brag about the battles they were in… Oh Jake, if only those boys knew."

Clayton had heard enough and he slid his feet off the desk, then said,

"Git outa this room now Wallace before I kill yah where yah stand."

"Well I heard you're goin' up to Petersburg next week Jake. I'm never gonna see yah agin. I've been to see the surgeon the other day, with the other two boys we came up here with Jake… The good news is, the other boy's wounds are healin' just fine, just fine. But my eye has turned bad, real bad and the surgeon tells me I ain't got that long to live, I got gangrene and I'm gonna die real soon Jake. So that's why I came to see yah Jake, just to say goodbye to an old comrade in arms…"

Clayton did not even try to conceal his delight on hearing this and sneered,

"Well I'm sure you'll be surprised to hear that I'm just real glad to hear that news Wallace. Now git your ass outa this office now, or you'll die a lot quicker than you thought you were gonna, now git."

Jed just adjusted his eye patch, chuckled again and said,

"You'll have a brand new audience for all your stories and lies up at Petersburg Jake, a whole new audience… I've seen some real bad fella's in this war Jake, some real scum, real scum. And that scum always comes to the surface in the end Jake… And fella's like you are the ferment of that scum Clayton."

Clayton kicked his chair back and blundered around the desk to get at Jed. He didn't even see the knife as Jed whipped it from behind his back and plunged it to the hilt into Clayton's stomach. He was dead before he even fell to the floor. Jed pulled the knife clean out from Clayton's stomach as he slumped down and muttered,

"Yah won't be goin' up to Petersburg Jake, yah won't be goin' to Petersburg."

As Wayne approached the stables he wondered what had happened. There were boys milling about looking for somebody, or something. He had just left Belinda by the well and there was no sign of anything else unusual going on around the camp. So what was going on around the stables. Then as he got closer he could see the Provost Marshall and two deputies talking with Luke. His immediate thoughts were that the militia had discovered Luke's secret past and had put a warrant out for his arrest. But those thoughts were soon cast aside as the Provost Marshall and the deputies saw him approaching and rapidly walked towards him. The Marshall produced a piece of paper, held it out for Wayne to see and said,

"Private Rawlins, Private Wayne Rawlins, I have a warrant for your arrest... You are under suspicion of murdering a Private Jake Clayton while he was carrying out his duties in the jailhouse. I have reason to believe there has been another incident concerning yourself and Private Clayton. On investigation it would appear that you have inflicted injuries on Private Clayton before, so you are the prime suspect."

Wayne was still scratching his head and trying to gather his thoughts when a voice interrupted the proceedings. It was the hoarse, rasping voice of Jed Wallace.

"They'll be no need to arrest Private Rawlins Marshall, it was me, I did it. I killed Jake Clayton in cold blood... I planned it and executed it and I couldn't of done a better job... I'm sorry, so sorry... I never wanted to kill a man in my life and

I've killed many. I've seen the blood of so many good, brave boys spilled for what, what in the end. I never wanted to fight, but I did… And now I must pay the price, pay the price."

He unwrapped a twelve inch knife from a blood stained handkerchief and held it up by the blade for the Marshall to see and said,

"Here's the murder weapon Marshall, I think that's all the evidence you'll need."

As the deputies clamped his bony old wrists in handcuffs he looked at Wayne and said,

"God bless yah Wayne, God be with yah for the rest of yah life… I want yah to know I've never met a better man, throughout this whole terrible damn war."

Wayne felt a hand clasp his arm. It was Luke and he was looking into Wayne's face with tears in his eyes. Wayne's head was still spinning in bewilderment as Luke said, "Are you okay Wayne?"

"Sure I'm okay Luke. We'd better git some shuteye… The Colonel tells me they're bringin' in some more hosses in the mornin' and we'll have work to do."

CHAPTER 17

Belinda was sitting between Wayne's legs, overlooking the same view where they had made love in carefree abandon the day before.

"When did yah stop believin' Wayne? What was it that turned you into a doubting Thomas? There musta been a time, a turnin' point for yah."

Wayne had his head propped up on the top of her head, gazing out over the river. His mind had been somewhere else and it took him some time to digest and answer her question. She was beginning to wonder if he had heard her when he replied.

"Doubtin' Thomas, never been called that before, s'pose that's as close as you could git to what I am...I quite like it. Maybe on my grave-stone they should carve – Here lies Wayne Rawlins – Doubting Thomas, who just couldn't understand what the preacher meant when he said he must suffer and sacrifice to be redeemed."

"So it all started when you were young then, even before war broke out," said Belinda.

Again Wayne had to think carefully and digest the question by turning it over.

"Well I look at it like this... Yah go to school, yah learn to read and write... It may take some time and some learn faster than others... But when yah finally grasp what the teacher's bin teachin' yah, what you've got is somethin' substantial. Yah can see what that teacher has bin aimin' for and what he has bin tryin' to make yah understand... Just like mathematics, it's just the same... Some may learn faster than others, but in the end yah can see how that mathematical equation adds up... like three plus four plus five equals twelve... Now with the Preacher, when we had to go to church on Sunday, I could never understand what he was gettin' at... Now why should folks be grateful for the food on their table, when they've bin workin' all day in the fields to put that food on the table? Now why should we feel guilty 'bout things we like, when we ain't hurtin', robbin' or doin' anythin' bad to our neighbours.

And why should we be aware of damnation and punishment, when all we're really tryin' to do is survive and go about our business. I just cannot, and have never bin able to understand it. It beats me."

Belinda laughed and pulled his knees together, squeezing her sides.

"You sure are one big doubtin' Thomas Wayne...Did the preacher ever tell yah that the Lord moves in strange ways? And is behind things beyond our understandin'?"

"He did, he did, but that still don't make sense to me. For example, when a boy sees a fine lookin' gal, why the hell should he feel guilty and dirty 'bout those feelin's? Why the hell should he feel inclined to go and take a cold bath to cool his damn ardour, as our damn fool preacher would call it... I don't even know what ardour means, so how the hell can yah cool somethin' yah don't even know the damn meanin' of?"

"It means something akin to what we feel for each other Wayne, only it's not a word I would use. Because it debases somethin' which is far deeper and more personal."

"Then I must be really damn ardour and I don't feel in the least guilty 'bout it."

Belinda could not hide her hilarity of Wayne's cool, calculating logic. But when he went into a deep, thoughtful mode, he explained his logic in the only way he could.

"Firstly I lose my Ma and the preacher tells my Pa that she was taken by God, but he couldn't explain why... I lose mah brother Wyatt, who wouldn't say boo to a goose. I lose my friends Ty and Wade... Who, when I watched them walk away down that road, never believed that they were never comin' back. I can still remember all of those boys, some proud in their smart grey uniforms... And some like Ty and Wade, laughin' and jokin' and kickin' each other up the ass... And some like Wyatt, lookin' around at all the fine ladies and dandy dudes, not knowin' that they were really goin' to fight a rich man's war, that was to be written in the blood of poor men. Boys better than any damn plantation owner or some damn fool preacher. Why did they all have to die, why?"

Belinda could feel his heart beating rapidly through her back and leaned back by pulling his knees back and shifting her position towards him. He carried on speaking.

"I wish I could change everythin', but I can't, I wish I could bring back Wyatt, Ty and Wade, but I can't... I wish I could of stopped the order to fire on Fort Sumter... I wish I'd never heard my Pa say the day it happened – Now the hand that has been hoverin' above us, waitin' to strike us, has bin given the reason it has bin just lookin' for, to come down on us, with a hammer in that hand onto our heads. – I wished I'd never stuck a bayonet in a boy that I never knew. I wish I'd never shot a boy that was no different from me. And through all of this I have to listen to some preacher, who talks in riddles and expects us to know what the hell he's talking 'bout. Well I don't, I never have and I never will… I ain't the only one who thinks that way… Why do we have to have some ole fool Padre attached to our regiments to bless us when we're about to kill and be killed…? I can remember after Sharpsburg. We had been holdin' a sunken road when the Federals attacked us in force… We knocked back wave after wave of assaults. There were Federals piled up and strewn across the fields in front of us. A whole cornfield had been cropped right down to the roots by our firing… The corn was soaked through with blood and still they kept comin'… They hit us with cannon fire, shot and canister, just to take that damn road… The road was piled high with our boys and we were standin' on their bodies bayonetin' and shootin' the Federal boys at point blank range as they came over… And after that battle where we had lost a lot of our best boys and Officers, we had to listen to, listen to a sermon by some damned ole Padre, tellin' us we are gonna go to hell for our crimes and killin'… We are gonna go to hell and suffer eternal damnation and the wrath of God will smite us with a heavy hand… And our Colonel finally lost his temper and shouted at him,

"All my boys are goin' to heaven you damned old blackguard, every single one of them is goin' to heaven and don't you forget it. They've suffered, sacrificed and died… Only damned ole fools like you should go to hell…

Now git the hell outa here before I ram yah fire and brimstone up yah ass and boot your ass all the way to hell and back, now git…" And one of the boys shouted to the Colonel, –

"Very nice sermon Colonel you've sure missed your true vocation." –

I can remember at Gettysburg when we came back down from Cemetery ridge, runnin' for our lives. We could see the cannon balls flyin' past us, between us and over our heads and the bang and the whizzin' could only be heard long after the cannon balls had passed and ripped holes in our rear guard… And I can remember tryin' to escape after the battle with Federal patrols tryin' to cut us off and shootin' at us as we crossed a river. And I can still see the Padre from General Pickets brigade, swim across the river fully clothed, even beatin' the horses to the other bank. Then jump clean over a fence and run for his life like lightnin', with all the boys laughin' and shoutin' – 'Look at him run, look at the Padre run, he's runnin' like the devil himself.' – I can remember at Malvern Hill when we were ordered to attack massed Federal artillery, which was coverin' their retreat from Harrison's landing… The fire was so heavy that nobody could even stand up without being beheaded, cut clean in half, or blown to pieces by the thousands… I used to pine and pray that it was some kind of nightmare and I would wake up from it. I would wake up back home, ridin' out in the wilds on mah hoss Long Horn, with only the wind through the trees and the sound of the river as company… And I can still see the look of pity on all their faces when they heard I was being drafted out to the east…Twenty two faces, twenty two lives that were marchin' away to fanfares and ladies in white frocks, wavin' their handkerchiefs around… Twenty two faces who thought I was bein' sent away to die on some unknown battlefield… And I still can't believe I'm here and all twenty two of them are dead…"

CHAPTER 18

The General and the telegrapher.

For the third time that day the telegrapher knocked on the General's door, walked in and handed the General a telegraph. The General took the telegraph and read it carefully then read it again to make sure he had read it correctly. He then stood up, towering over the telegrapher and said,

"Have you read the contents of this Saunders."

"Yes I have Sir and I knew that you'd want it right away."

"Has anybody else read it Saunders?"

"No Sir, I know that all telegraphs that come in are to come directly to you."

"Have you told anybody about the subject matter of this Saunders."

"No Sir, I came straight here as soon as it finished comin' through."

"Under no circumstances talk, or even mention this to anybody Saunders, or I'll have your guts for garters, I promise you."

The telegrapher could not hide his fear, because the General could be extremely intimidating to anybody, in particular, a mild mannered telegrapher who knew him.

"You have my word Sir, I will not even speak to anybody else about it."

"Good Saunders, good. We must keep this between us and us alone, because panic and mutiny could erupt in the ranks if this news is known before I have thought out how I'm gonna break it to the boys… If anything else comes in, anything, bring it to me, even if it's in the middle of the night. You do realise the gravity of this news Saunders?"

"I do Sir, I do… But are you surprised Sir? If you don't mind me askin'?"

"No Saunders, no. And I hope Leopold Blunt can accept my humble apologies."

"Leopold Blunt Sir?"

The General looked out through the window, across the dusty courtyard and said,

"Never mind Saunders, never mind, you can go."

With that they exchanged sharp salutes and Saunders left. The General went back to his desk, opened a draw and pulled out a bottle of whisky and a tumbler. He poured himself a large measure, held it up and said,

"Here's to you Leopold, I wish you were here, I wish you were here."

The next day as the General was pawing over his latest despatches and various miscellaneous telegraphs that were strewn across his desk, a loud and heavy-handed knock came at the door. Saunders almost burst into the room, saluted and handed a telegraph to the General, who couldn't fail to notice the alarmed manner of Saunders.

"Good mornin' Sir. This has just come in and I knew you'd want it right away."

"Very good Saunders."

The General carefully read the telegraph twice and said,

"Right Saunders, right. The same as I told you yesterday, don't mention this to anybody. This news is real bad Saunders, real bad."

"Yes Sir, but I'd better tell you that another one's comin' through at this very moment. I locked the office before I came over… It should be ready when I get back."

"Go and get it Saunders and bring it to me as quick as you can."

When Saunders came back the knock that rapped on the door was so soft that the General barely heard it. This time Saunders face was white with shock as he handed the telegraph to the General. The General read it, but he was not prepared for what was in the contents. He put it down on the desk, put his head in his hands and muttered,

"My God, my God! What do I do now Leopold? Tell me… What do I do now?"

Luke felt a strong hand clasp his shoulder as he pitchforked hay into the horse troughs. He knew it was Wayne before he even turned around, but he had not been expecting him this early. Wayne's manner was serious and he spoke to Luke in earnest.

"Mornin' Luke, glad to see you've fed and watered the hosses early today."

"Mornin' Wayne, yeh, it saves me doin' it later, there's more to attend to now."

"Now Luke, I want yah to listen to me carefully and do exactly what I tell yah."

Luke had never experienced Wayne behaving this way before and became slightly worried. But he had learnt to trust Wayne implicitly and would do anything for him.

"Okay Wayne, whatever yah want, I'll do it right away, no problems."

"Right, feed groom and water the young black stallion Luther, the brown and white Red wind and the female you said that Belinda took a shinin' to…Also choose three more, two female one male and make sure they're strong and healthy, I'll let you choose them yaself… Make sure they're all well rested… Take two muskets, two pistols and the big shotgun from my room and clean them thoroughly… I want all the barrels reamed out with linseed… Then stow plenty of ammunition for them, ready to load up onto the hosses… Then take the corn bread, rice and hardtack I've bin storin' and bag it up… Then make sure that plenty of water is bottled up for us and the hosses… As soon as I give the word tomorrow afternoon, load everythin' up onto the hosses that you have chosen, all three of them. The three that we'll be ridin' must be carryin' as little as possible, they may be in for a long, hard haul. Belinda will be helpin' yah, I've just gotta talk to her first… Take all the hosses and cross the river in the shallows, near where the women do their washin'… Make yah way up to the high ground on the other side of the river, overlookin' the camp… Then just wait for me."

Only now did Luke feel inclined to ask Wayne the reason for these calculated instructions. And he knew Wayne never did anything without good reasons.

"What's happened Wayne? Are we in trouble? Has the militia caught up with me?"

"No Luke, but I've got a hunch and I'm sure I'm right… The General has only come out of his office twice in three days. He's even sleepin' in there… He's sent his horse Jubal over for us to look after and he hasn't even come over to see if Jubal is okay… The telegrapher Saunders has bin back and forth between the telegraph office and the Generals… I've never seen so many telegraphs flyin' around and we're only a very small contingent… And Saunders is lookin' as white as a ghost and he ain't bin talkin' to anybody… He ain't even bin goin' to the nightly gatherin's and I know he's never missed them in the past… Saunders knows somethin' and he's bin told not to tell anybody… And when the General tells somebody to jump they say how high, not why…" He then put his hands on Luke's shoulders, with his sky blue eyes boring into Luke's.

"Yah must do what I say Luke, I'm dependin' on yah. I think I know why Saunders is as white as a ghost and ain't talkin' to anybody… And I'm sure I know why the General dare not move far from his office… He'll be talkin' to all the boys 'bout five o'clock tomorrow afternoon… But I'm hopin' that there's only one piece of bad news, coz when Saunders left the General's office 'bout an hour ago, he staggered back to the telegraph office as if he had just swallowed a whole bottle of whisky and I've never seen him drink in four years… Somethin' very serious has happened Luke, I can feel it."

He then turned and strode away, jumping clean over a bucket as he went through the stable door. Now came the hard part, he must talk to Belinda and persuade her that his plans for the three of them were the best, if not the only option. In his heart it had become his dire duty to look after and protect Belinda and Luke at all costs.

Belinda had been listening to Wayne intently, her high cheekbones were glistening with moisture and her long eyelashes were occasionally fluttering around like butterflies trying to land over her big, brown eyes. When Wayne had finished talking she said,

"So you really think that all of these telegraphs that have been coming through over the past few days, could really be carryin' the news that the war's lost."

"Could be, but I can't understand why the General is hangin' on to tell the boys… I've been ponderin' a whole lotta things… If General Lee has been killed then that means disaster for us… He's the only one who could negotiate a peace that would hinder and stop any form of reprisals against us… Even our damn fool Politicians who dragged us into this war in the first place know that… If the Federals have broken the Petersburg lines and captured Richmond, then we'll be just as good as beaten anyway… If General Sherman can corner and crush General Johnston's army, which is lookin' more and more likely… Then that would give Sherman a clear road, straight up through this very camp, to come up from behind on Lee's already battered army, and he and General Grant can crush Lee at their own leisure… As I've just told you, I'm not lettin' you and Luke stay around here anyway… I want yah to wait with Luke tomorrow afternoon until I've heard what the General's gotta say and I've gotta hunch we may have to move real fast… There's somethin' 'bout the way the General's actin' that's worryin' me."

Belinda's look had become pensive and slightly apprehensive as she asked Wayne,

"Well don't you think we could take our chances surrenderin' to the Federals Wayne? After all my father did fight and die for their cause, surely they would show us mercy."

"Well Belinda, I sure wish I could share your faith of our fellow man, but I don't. If nothin' else this war has taught me how cruel and barbaric any man can be under certain circumstances… I'm not just worried 'bout the Federals, but our own damn militia. I simply don't wanna leave you, Luke or even my damn self at the mercy of, I don't know what… If our militia get hold of you or Luke, you're both as good as dead and they're prowlin' around just to the south of here, well behind General Johnston's lines…

The Federals may, or may not treat us well, that's if they don't kill the whole damn camp outa revenge. Our boys might even decide to fight to the last man, coz they're gonna die anyway. I simply don't know what's gonna happen… But I'm prepared for the worse and I've planned everythin' real carefully… Federals to the north east, probably marchin' this way at this very moment… Our militia between General Johnston and another massive Federal army just to the south west, that's poised to crush General Johnston's already patched up army; built outa other broken armies. Now if we move out, in a straight line west, over the river and through the mountain passes, we should give everybody the slip. There's plenty of streams and rivers out that way and it's the only area where there's no maraudin' Federals, or Reb patrols."

Belinda still looked anxious, but just like Luke she had learned to trust Wayne implicitly. And Wayne sensing her doubts, completely swung her around to his plans as he put his hands onto her shoulders and said in exasperation,

"This time I'm no doubtin' Thomas Belinda, I gotta hunch that somethin' real bad has happened… It's as clear as spring water…Why, even my good brother Wyatt in all o' his wisdom would agree with me, if he was here."

She put her head onto his chest, wrapped her arms around him and looked up at him.

"Okay Wayne, I'll meet Luke by the stables tomorrow and help him load up… I've never known a more honest doubtin' Thomas than you."

CHAPTER 19

A General, a speech and a long shadow.

The stage was set for the General's speech. The boys that knew him, in particular the ones of a higher standard of education could appreciate the eloquence and sense of drama of how the old man could deliver his speeches. He had always had the ability to lift the heaviest heart, even after a particularly ferocious and bloody battle with superb, yet conciliatory praise. But today everybody knew that it would be different. Everybody in their hearts knew that today he would be the bringer of bad news. They were all meandering around the dusty square talking nervously, some occasionally glancing between the podium and the General's office door.

Everything went deadly quiet when that door opened and the General stepped out onto the porch. Today he was in his full military regalia, with black, knee length riding boots, long white gauntlets, a golden sash and his marvellous, long sword fixed to his belt. In one hand he held a leather satchel of ordered dispatches and the other his grey, broad brimmed hat. His orderly and Saunders only stepped out onto the porch when they saw that the General was about to move. Wayne was at the back of the gathering and of all the boys that were watching the old man intently, he was the one with the deepest feeling of trepidation in his heart. The General slowly walked down the four steps, causing the sound of four blunt thuds, which echoed around the austere and ramshackle buildings. His big, bowlegs carried him across the square in casual strides with Saunders and the orderly having to move rapidly to fall into step, either side of him.

He only put his hat on after he had climbed onto the podium and waited for Saunders and the orderly to move around either side of the podium. He dwarfed both of them anyway and his stance on the podium made him appear like a giant to them. Some of the boys had noticed that the relatively cocksure and confident Saunders had begun to sway about like a thin sapling in the wind. Only there was no wind.

Only silence and a long dark shadow, which the General was casting over the gathering, by some trick of the late afternoon sun. A grey man, with grey hair and a beard, in a grey uniform, casting a long dark shadow over men who had suffered and sacrificed for far too long.

He rifled through his satchel and pulled out a long dispatch and looked out over his dumbstruck audience. The brim of his hat covered his eyes and he was completely unaware of his own grand posture and countenance. He began to speak and his voice echoed around the outbuildings, as if it was descending on the gathering from all sides.

"Gentlemen, friends, brothers in arms…I have been meaning to speak to you for three days now. But I have been overwhelmed by a whole string of dispatches and incoming telegraphs… I have had to delay this meeting, until I could put all of these dispatches and telegraphs into some format in which I can give you a full, complete and comprehensive picture of unexpected events… which, which have happened…"

Wayne noticed that Saunders nearly fell over and the orderly stepped back to control his balance. The anxious feeling of the unknown was replaced by the cold, clasping fear of something too terrible to comprehend, which swept through Wayne's emotions and he could feel it descend onto the whole gathering. He glanced around at the ten General Officers who were standing at either side of the podium and gauging by the look on their faces, none of them had an inkling about what was in the contents of the dispatches. The General then pulled a pair of half moon glasses from his top pocket then cleaned them delicately with a handkerchief. The tension was simply too much for Saunders who suddenly buckled down onto his knees and fell forward into the dust. Two officers, who were standing close by, immediately went to his aid.

The General did not even appear to notice the prostrate Saunders as he looked around in long sweeps, scanning the whole gathering to draw attention to himself.

"Three days ago, our own General Lee surrendered to General Grant at a hamlet about twenty miles to the north east of here called, Appomattox Court House."

There was a muffled and garbled gasp, which rolled forth from the whole gathering, which echoed around the outbuildings as if it was trying to escape into the ether. The old man waited patiently for the news to be digested by all, before he carried on.

"Our great Commander had no other alternative than to surrender."

Shouts of, 'They ain't got us yet Sir, we'll fight 'em to the death' and, 'We'll fight to the last man, if yah want us to Sir,' were quickly quelled by one long sweep of the General's arm, with the palm of his gauntlet moving in a wide arch.

"Friends, good loyal friends, we cannot carry on. I have received orders from General Lee himself that all hostilities are to cease forthwith and I am to surrender the entire camp to the first Federal Commander who arrives here. You all have known for a long time that we have been losing this war for months... The fear that the Federals would break through the Petersburg lines and capture Richmond has finally come to pass... The hope that our great and noble Commander, who has always turned the tables in the past could pull something off like he has always done in the past, well that hope has been lost forever... He did try to break away and drive his army southwest to join General Johnston, but that also failed. His supply trains had been overrun and ransacked by Federal cavalry, under General Sheridan. All of the rails approaching and leaving Lynchburg have been ripped up. His men were collapsing from exhaustion and starvation along the way. His horses were dropping dead and their loads were having to be carried by the men... He fought until all hope was gone. When the road had been cut off in front of him at Appomattox, he had been completely surrounded on three sides and outnumbered eight to one... The whole of the Federal V. Corps, IV. Corps and II Corps had been brought up to their full strengths. Their Generals Meade, Gibbon, Ord, and Humphrey's have been driving them for thirty five miles a day, to flank and head General Lee off... He simply could not stage an effective battle, with low ammunition against over a hundred thousand Federals, with artillery and massed cavalry probing all around him. He could not turn things round this time, not this time."

Once again he let his stunned audience take stock of this news before carrying on. But this time his voice had moved up into a clear and precise piece of oratory.

"Friends, brave boys, there is a lot more, a lot more. Please try to bear with me and listen… There has been a terrible battle at Bentonville. Our General Johnston has inflicted terrible causalities on Federal General Slocum. He attacked the left flank of General Slocum's army, taking him completely by surprise. However he could not press home with the attack, because General Sherman sent in reinforcements. Although he put up a terrible fight, he was completely outnumbered. He held them off by forming an arrow like formation and desperately tried to break General Sherman's army in half. If he had done this, then there still may have been a chance for us to carry on for a while, but our resources and supplies are so thin now we can barely feed the remainder of our armies. General Sherman's army has now joined up with General Schofield's at Goldsboro, North Carolina and their combined armies' number around possibly over a hundred thousand men… General Johnston was forced to retreat to stop himself from being outflanked and surrounded… That is where he received dispatches that General Lee had surrendered to General Grant. That is when he called a truce with General Sherman to discuss terms of surrender for his own army. General's Grant and Sherman have offered both General's Lee and Johnston very similar terms."

Once again the General allowed plenty of time for this news to be digested by his men. But Wayne knew in his heart that there was something else that the General had been holding back, because he had grown to know the old man from four long years of serving under him… And he always held the worse news back right to the last.

"Friends, my boys, my brave, loyal boys… Generals Grant and Sherman have negotiated very generous terms for us… In effect, we only have to hand our munitions, muskets and any articles for conducting war over to them, and obey the paroles, laws and rules of the Federal Government… and, and we will be left alone by that Government.

General's Grant and Sherman have conducted themselves with the greatest regard, sense of duty and honour… They have both cut, confounded and broken any chances of reprisals, revenge and hangings, from the ravenous, angry men in power that are baying for our blood, by implementing these terms. These terms are what Mister Lincoln himself wanted, they were the deepest wish of Mister Lincoln himself."

The General scanned the gathering with his eyes covered by the broad brim of his hat. His shadow by now had extended far past the gathering and appeared to be painted on the wall of an outbuilding, rising up out of the dusty square. The boys began to talk amongst themselves, if not in relief; then glad in the knowledge that the Federal Generals had been merciful to a vanquished foe. And brought the war to a close by not the swing of a hammer, or by the stroke of a sword, but by the putting of pen to paper. Wayne noticed that the General had spoken quietly to his orderly, who was standing on tiptoes to hear what the old man was saying, as he bent down from the podium. The orderly quickly rifled through his pouch and produced a long, white telegraph and handed it to the General… The General walked back to the centre of the podium in two long strides and called everybody to attention once again. The boys looked around at each other and wondered what else could have happened. He looked down at the paper in his hand, then began to lift it, as though he was lifting and balancing a great weight in his hand… Wayne felt as though he had been punched in the solar plexus as the old man said in a broken, emotional voice,

"Gentlemen, I did not tell you this piece of news before, because it came in just after General Johnston had surrendered to General Sherman... President Lincoln has been murdered. He was shot through the head as he sat in his private box, in the Ford theatre in Washington... He died shortly after the event, I'm so sorry to have to tell you this."

There was a slightly delayed reaction and then a loud, audible gasp of horror swept across the whole multitude of dumbstruck men. The General carried on speaking.

"Generals Sherman and Johnston received the telegraph right in the middle of negotiating terms and conditions of surrender... General Sherman immediately sent all of his troops back to camp in Raleigh... And kept the whole debacle a secret until he could send out a dispatch to all of his troops, breaking that news in the best way he could... In that dispatch he informed them that this fiendish, dastardly deed had been carried out by villains of unknown motives, or intentions. He has categorically stated that in no way or circumstance has any Confederate Officer, soldier, member of the Confederate Government had any dealings, or operation in this deplorable act of cold blooded murder... The assassins name is John Wilkes Booth, but he is the only one who pulled the trigger. There are believed to be at least five or six other perpetrators in this crime... All of our Generals and members of Congress are condemning this despicable crime, which could only have dire consequences for our whole cause. Very fortunately for us, General Grant should have been in the same private box as Mister Lincoln, but he had been called urgently to Petersburg when a breakthrough became imminent... Thank God he missed an assassin's bullet thank God...!"

Wayne's immediate thoughts were how would the Federal soldiers treat them now? Because from what he could gather from the boys who guarded the prisoners, most of them had a very high regard for Mister Lincoln. He also knew that the names Thaddeus Stevens, Zachariah Chandler and Ben Wade were names synonymous with the bitter-enders that held office in Mister Lincoln's cabinet. And had made no secret to Mister Lincoln, or anybody else that the rebellion should be put down with a heavy hand and without mercy. But Wayne's fears were alleviated a little when the General drew their attention again and a deathly silence descended on the gathering once again.

"May I have your attention again please gentlemen... An emergency meeting has been called by the Federal Government and fortunately for us Secretary of war Mister Edwin Stanton has been nominated to stand in for Mister Lincoln, until they can democratically nominate somebody else. Hopefully by then things will quieten down."

A deep sigh of relief rose from the gathering, but the General was far from finished.

"Now it's my turn to speak to you all personally, all of you... And I want to talk to you on a personal level and not as your commanding officer... A General's job is not an easy one, far from it... Nor is that of a soldier... Indeed we have so much in common... I know that all of you are the remnants of three separate regiments... And I know that all of you are very proud of those regiments... All of you have fought in some of the most terrible battles this country will ever see... Each of your regiments numbered to over a thousand when they were formed, at the start of the war... And now the remainder of those regiments amount to just over two hundred and sixty combined, combined..."

The General gagged as if he was trying to fight back tears, but he carried on.

"All of you have served our cause above and beyond the call of duty... At one stage, as indeed in many stages throughout this war victory came so close, so close. But it was always snatched right from under our noses... As all of you have seen that the traffic of supplies and men have dwindled to practically nothing going up to the battle fronts. And more and more traffic has been coming back through, broken, battered and lost. I know that when war was declared very few of you had ever even seen a musket, let alone fire one... I know that your tools were tools of the land, the plough, the hoe, the pitchfork, the spade and wagon... Tools for planting, harvesting, and reaping the fruits of your toil, fruits of the land... These tools were rudely ripped from your hands and replaced by tools of war, the musket, the bayonet and the dreadful artillery piece."

Once again the General gagged, putting his head forward as if his hat could cover the emotion and trauma that he was going through.

"When, when you were all called to volunteer, your lives were not much better, or just as bad as the slaves who you worked the land with... Very few of you had any quarrel or bad feelings towards these poor fellows whose lot was basically the same as yours.

Fellows that worked the land just like yourself with plough, hoe, pitchfork and spade. Planting and harvesting cotton, wheat and grain... Rhetoric and speeches of throwing out the northern invader, and your state rights are being overruled by forces outside of your states, didn't really warn you of the dire consequences of putting aside your tools of the land and replacing them with tools of war. Gentlemen, over the last few weeks I have been given orders to send most of you to the front and help man the Petersburg lines... I have countermanded all of those orders, by delaying and sending dispatches to the high command that I need you all here... If we had to go, we would go together, fight together and die together... You have all done far more than I could ever ask from you and I may be your commanding officer, but I am also your humble and grateful servant. Just like yourselves, I thought this war would come to a fast close."

He paused for a while and drew in a long, deep breath before continuing,

"I thought that there would be a lot of sabre rattling, a lot of angry posturing and a lot of urgent and desperate meetings to avoid all out war, I was wrong, wrong. All of you have seen men die and all of you have killed. All of you have seen your friends and comrades lives snatched from them in the most horrible manner. I dare say their faces and voices still haunt you. Many years before this terrible shadow swept across this beautiful, fertile land I was warned that it would happen. At the time I dismissed such beliefs as nonsense and fatalistic pessimism and that dismissal has been thrown back in my face on every single battlefield. That discussion would of happened when most of you were no more than young children, scampering barefoot, through meadow and field. All of you could never of known that the silly girls giggling at you, at the time, would never grow into blushing brides, waiting for amorous sweethearts, but sad and lonely widows. A lot of them would never hear the sound of wedding bells, but the slow chime of the funeral bell. My good friend, the good Reverend Leopold Blunt had been right with all of his predictions, as we sat around his table discussing religion and theology. He was right, so right.

I could never agree with the cantankerous old swine on much, because our views collided from most aspects. He believed in his heart that all men are born the same and are all children of God. Whether you are white, Indian, or black slave, it simply did not matter. I would always say that if your divine and noble God was in charge of the way man is, then why does he allow such injustice and inequality for his beloved children? His answer was always the same. The Devil can move, can move within the hearts of guilty men… He can hide, sneak around, lie, cheat and bear false witness within the human heart and soul… His cunning and fiendishness knows no bounds. He would tell me, you are a military man Ambrose and I know that you believe in justice, law and order, rules and written decrees that prevent criminal and political skulduggery, and uphold great and noble causes. And you as a military man, as your duty are there to enforce those laws if they are infringed and broken. Even if you have to die doing so, even if you have to die. When the good Reverend died suddenly and I was collecting and storing his papers with my wife, I happened to find a poem written in his own hand, which was hidden in an old bible. I took the liberty of taking it for myself and have kept it on my person ever since. On every battlefield, each gruelling march and every time we bury our dead. I would like to take the liberty of reading it to you. Because it was written for you my brave boys, written just for you, by a man you never knew. A man who died when you were still young children, a man who died, knowing what would happen to you."

He took a paper from his top pocket, cleaned his glasses and began to read, loudly.

Where are you going young man, with that tattered flag?
Where are you going young man, with that battered bag?
Have you left a lover, or have you left a wife?
How you make me shudder, the way you take that knife.
Why put that round in your breach, to shoot at targets out of reach?
Did you forsake your bride-to-be and leave her by the door?
Her breath still hangs in the air, while your dust blows on her floor.
Why are you crying young man, while looking at your corpse?
Why are you dying young man, drowning in remorse?
Because the hand that rocked your cradle, never dug your grave.
An epitaph with no name is where your spirit lays, is where your spirit lays…

He carefully folded the paper and slipped it back into his pocket, then turned to leave, he had nothing left to say… A deadly silence descended over the entire gathering. It was the General's darkest hour and yet his finest. His boys could now at last see him in his full glory. He had been released. This man who had driven and cajoled them on terrible battlefronts had suffered beyond all of their comprehension. The universal feeling towards him was akin to a child that was about to lose a father and that child had finally realised that his father had cared for and given protection as best as he possibly could in the circumstances. They could now see him for who he really was. And as he stepped down from the podium and handed his bag to his orderly, the roar of approval was so loud that it echoed out through the outbuildings and resounded around the mountains... Wayne found himself shouting and clapping with the rest of the boys despite himself... Some of them turned and hugged each other, some turned to shake hands with their nearest comrade and some just openly wept. But before this grey man, in a grey uniform, with a grey beard and hair could leave this stage forever, he was swept off his feet and into the air by officers and men alike. Wayne would have joined in, but he had other business to attend to and he had to move fast.

CHAPTER 20

The call of the hallowed wind.

Luke and Belinda were becoming anxious. They had done exactly what Wayne had told them to do and were wondering what had delayed him. They could see the gathering in the distance, far below them. Whatever the old General had been saying to them he was certainly taking a long time about it. Their vantage point was situated right on the top of a hill, with trees and bracken in abundance on the slopes in front of them and the same on the reclining slopes behind them… They were sitting between two old oak trees, mounted on their chosen horses and the three packhorses and Wayne's were tethered to those trees. Luke had begun to wonder if perhaps he and Belinda were so well hidden that Wayne could not find them. But no, he said here and here he meant, here. Luke had noticed that Belinda was becoming uneasy like himself and said,

"He did say here Belinda, didn't he? I'm sure he said here."

"He did Luke, maybe he's been held up for some reason…"

Before she could finish her sentence, something caught her attention, moving in the shrubbery on the other side of the river. Whatever it was, she lost sight of it as she tried to target her vision on the area. There it was again, and they both saw it at the same time. Yes it was Wayne's blond head, moving through tiny breaks in the clearings and disappearing and then reappearing from under the trees.

"There he is!" They both said in unison.

Luke breathed a deep sigh of relief and Belinda felt; well, Belinda felt the only way any woman would feel, when a woman is completely and utterly in love with a man.

Wayne finally negotiated and cleared the maze of trees and bracken and appeared by the banks of the river, then walked along the bank and began to cross at the shallows. When he finally arrived at their position, he looked around to check that they had followed his instructions and loaded up the horses correctly.

He was slightly out of breath and Belinda noticed the heavy atmosphere of melancholy in his countenance. Luke was the first to speak, but he already knew the answer to his own question.

"Well, what did the General say Wayne? Has the war bin lost?"

"Yep, but it's bin lost in a way that nobody could of expected. God help us, if there is a God and I sure hope that God can hear us... Sure glad it's Grant's boys that got us."

He untethered the three packhorses, then his own. He swung up casually onto the back of his horse and positioned himself between Belinda and Luke. As he did so the thunder of hooves of massed cavalry and the yawning creak of artillery wheels could be heard in the distance. The three of them looked out over towards the distant hills and mountain roads that loomed up from behind the camp. Firstly came the cavalry, streaming down the hillsides like blue fingers of rivulets, probing and darting down towards the camp. Then over the mountain roads came the massed Federal infantry and artillery. And then to announce the mighty blue host came a massed band playing, 'The Campbell's are coming', in swanky, cocksure abandon. Belinda noticed that Wayne looked relieved, rather than perplexed or frightened. She found out why when he said,

"They're coming in from the north east, good, good. That'll be Grant's boys. Thank God that Sherman's boys didn't get here first. Right it's time for us to move out."

But just before he pulled his horse away he was suddenly distracted. Down in the camp he could see two figures moving out towards the mighty, military host. It was the General, perched on his horse Jubal, with his orderly on another horse, carrying the Generals colours. Wayne let a wry smile creep across his face as he said,

"Now don't throw the good General Jubal… It sure ain't no time to embarrass him."

They moved down the slopes of the hill, weaving and ducking through the trees. Wayne was not pushing them to move fast, because they had a long way to go.

As they slowly climbed up the steep sides of another heavily wooded hill, Belinda knew the view, which would confront them as they reached the top. She was right. As they broke through the final barricade of bush and bracken, there it was, in all of its panoramic glory. The blue mountain was a shade darker than it usually was and it appeared to be floating on a bright pink and violet cloud this time. The river far below was a deep indigo, snaking its way towards the distant mountains. As they began to ride down the narrow, overgrown path that led down into the valleys Belinda gave Luke's horse a dig in the rear with her bare foot and began to giggle as Luke's horse lurched forward. Luke had to quickly steady himself, otherwise he would have been rudely dismounted.

"Whatyah doin' Belinda? I'm glad somebody feels like havin' fun, coz I sure don't. Whatyah tryin' to do, kill me or somethin'?" He said in mock anger.

Wayne thought to himself that even when she was in a mood for levity Belinda was graceful. Even when kicking a horse up the backside, she did it with grace.

Suddenly and quite inexplicably the faces of Wade, Ty and Wyatt appeared in his mind. He could feel Wade's ginger hair brush under his nose and chin and his strong hands clasp his waist, just like in one of their many boyish wrestling matches. He could see Ty's huge footprints leaving duck-like tracks in the dusty, winding path. He could feel the whiplash of the bracken and taste and smell the dust as he and Wade followed Ty. He could hear Ben Boucher's booming voice, 'HOW DARE YOU BRING DISRESPECT AND HUMILIATION INTO THE HOUSE OF THE LORD!' And quietly, just like a reassuring whisper he heard the voice of Wyatt, 'A damn fool dude Wayne, a damn fool dude.'

And his own voice answered Wyatt almost apologetically, 'A damn brave fool Wyatt, a damn brave fool.'

And as they moved down into the valley a warm wind suddenly swept up and around them, jostling the branches and rustling the leaves of the trees.

It circled them, then pushed and pulled them, ruffling their hair and rushing through their hearts and souls in unison. Was it the spirits of the thousands of dead that was greeting them? Or was it a hallowed wind of destiny that had come to collect them. And what was that feeling Wayne could sense. Yes, it was that feeling of wonder and longing, which he had spoken about with Belinda… But what was that other feeling in his heart. It was happiness. Yes it was happiness and after all of these years of loneliness and terrible suffering, he had finally discovered what it felt like to be happy. He looked down on Belinda and Luke in amusement, as they weaved their way down the path. Luke tried to shove Belinda's horse off the path with his own. Belinda easily avoided him, then kicked him up the backside and giggled. It dawned on Wayne that it was these two lost and dispossessed souls who had brought happiness to his door. It had crept in through the backdoors of his mind slowly but surely, like rapier beams of light through cracks in a dusty, opaque and broken window.

He closed his eyes and let the sound of Belinda's giggle and Luke's frustrated cursing sweep him away on a sea of emotions, breaking and dancing like thunderous, roaring waves on a distant sublime beach.